The Wild Card

Also From Dylan Allen

RIVERS WILDE SERIES OF STAND ALONE STORIES
Listed in suggested reading order

The Legacy
Book one of the Rivers Wilde Series. An opposites attract, enemies to lovers standalone that kicks off this brand new series.

The Legend
This is a second chance at love story. Remington Wilde has loved one woman in his life and even though timing and family manipulations keep pulling them apart, it's a love worth fighting for.

The Jezebel
Regan Wilde and Stone Rivers were born enemies. But love has other ideas. This sweeping, second chance romance spans nearly twenty years and will make you believe in soul mates.

The Daredevil: A Rivers Wilde/ 1001 Nights Novella
This story has all the hallmarks of Rivers Wilde—drama, sex, humor, heartwarming family interactions, and two amazingly driven, brilliant, bold characters who are also PERFECT for each other. A fake relationship, a weekend in Paris and all the feels.

The Mastermind: A Rivers Wilde Novella

SYMBOLS OF LOVE SERIES
Still the One
Then Came You
Best for Last
All for Love

STANDALONE NOVELS
The Sun and Her Star
Thicker Than Water
The Sound of Temptation

The Wild Card
A Rivers Wilde Novella
By Dylan Allen

1001 DARK NIGHTS
PRESS

The Wild Card
A Rivers Wilde Novella
By Dylan Allen

1001 Dark Nights

Copyright 2024 Dylan Allen
ISBN: 979-8-88542-063-1

Foreword: Copyright 2014 M. J. Rose

Published by 1001 Dark Nights Press, an imprint of Evil Eye Concepts, Incorporated

All rights reserved. No part of this book may be reproduced, scanned, or distributed in any printed or electronic form without permission. Please do not participate in or encourage piracy of copyrighted materials in violation of the author's rights.

This is a work of fiction. Names, places, characters and incidents are the product of the author's imagination and are fictitious. Any resemblance to actual persons, living or dead, events or establishments is solely coincidental.

Acknowledgments from the Author

The Wild Card is the first book I've written since a major surgery in December of 2021 that left me unable to drive, hold my children, or write for almost 6 months.

Returning to work was scary. My body and mind were rusty, my muses—out of shape.

We writers like to say that this is a solitary job. Well, the last few months have proven to me just how wrong that is.

It is thanks to the constant support of my family, friends and my 1001 Dark Nights family and my teams of editors, I crossed the finish line.

I don't know that I would have found the courage to attempt this story without Tijuana Turner, Kennedy Ryan, and Ann Jones constantly reminding that I could do it.

I'm not sure I would have even started writing this story without Lucy Eden and her trope bucket, or Carrie Ann Ryan sprinting with me.

My editor extraordinaire, Lauren McKellar took the convoluted stream of consciousness I sent her and helped me shape into this story.

Thank you to my agent, Lasheera Lee for believing in my vision.

A special word of gratitude belongs to Liz Berry and Stacey Tardif—thank you for helping me make this book shine.

Liz, MJ, and Jillian, I'm so grateful and honored to work with you. Thank you for giving me the opportunity to tell this story.

As always, none of the magic I weave would be possible without the support of my husband and children. The unwavering support of my parents and sisters and extended family continues to be the wind beneath my wings. As always, I am grateful to have the chance to write stories that entertain, provoke thought, and never leave you.

One Thousand and One Dark Nights

Once upon a time, in the future…

I was a student fascinated with stories and learning. I studied philosophy, poetry, history, the occult, and the art and science of love and magic. I had a vast library at my father's home and collected thousands of volumes of fantastic tales.

I learned all about ancient races and bygone times. About myths and legends and dreams of all people through the millennium. And the more I read the stronger my imagination grew until I discovered that I was able to travel into the stories… to actually become part of them.

I wish I could say that I listened to my teacher and respected my gift, as I ought to have. If I had, I would not be telling you this tale now. But I was foolhardy and confused, showing off with bravery.

One afternoon, curious about the myth of the Arabian Nights, I traveled back to ancient Persia to see for myself if it was true that every day Shahryar (Persian: شهریار, "king") married a new virgin, and then sent yesterday's wife to be beheaded. It was written and I had read that by the time he met Scheherazade, the vizier's daughter, he'd killed one thousand women.

Something went wrong with my efforts. I arrived in the midst of the story and somehow exchanged places with Scheherazade – a phenomena that had never occurred before and that still to this day, I cannot explain.

Now I am trapped in that ancient past. I have taken on Scheherazade's life and the only way I can protect myself and stay alive is to do what she did to protect herself and stay alive.

Every night the King calls for me and listens as I spin tales. And when the evening ends and dawn breaks, I stop at a point that leaves him breathless and yearning for more. And so the King spares my life for one more day, so that he might hear the rest of my dark tale.

As soon as I finish a story... I begin a new one... like the one that you, dear reader, have before you now.

1

Mission

CASSIE

"Hello from paradise," I grin into the camera, eyes wide, my arm waving at the endless blue sky at my back. "This is where I'll be working for the next week." I copy, paste and send the text to my parents, my brother, and my best friend. My fingers hover over my boyfriend Evan's name before I decide against it and slip my phone into my tote.

"Ugh," the pang of sadness that's replaced the gurgle of happiness I used to feel when I thought of him sucks.

Two weeks ago, he would have been the first person I texted. Now…I flinch at the memory of our last argument. His furious grimace, his barely contained rage and my helplessness in the face of it are still fresh in my mind. As is the realization that came in their aftermath—I had to leave him. He didn't touch me but the words he used were as violent as a fist to the face would have been. I'm not waiting to see if he does it again, or if it escalates.

Not even the financial security he'd introduced to my life could make up for feeling unsafe in my own home. Even if it means a temporary return to life on the wrong side of the law.

"Where is he?" I scan the long curb outside arrivals for my ride. There's a ball of nervous anticipation pulsing in my throat. I'm not sure what to expect when I see Michel again.

When I quit, he told me I'd come crawling back and laughed in my face before he hung up on me. I was sure then he was wrong. Unlike when he first recruited me, I didn't have my back against a financial wall.

Back then I was working three jobs to pay the shortfall in my tuition after all the grants and my athletic scholarship kicked in. My GPA suffered so much that I was kicked off the gymnastics team at the end of my freshman year. I couldn't make up the shortfall, my parents couldn't help me and I'd had no choice but to withdraw.

I was packing up my dorm room, preparing to leave school and move back to Houston when Michel called. He'd been one of the trainers at the gym where the university's athletes all worked out. We'd been friendly enough before he was fired for selling prescription Adderall on campus my freshman year. But I'd never given him my number.

He explained that he still had access to the school directory, had heard from one of the coaches I'd lost my scholarship and had a proposition that would help me stay in school.

We met for coffee at a place near campus and he explained what he needed.

He'd been working in private security since he left the university and was branching out into what he called asset retrieval. He needed someone with the strength and agility of a gymnast to carry out the actual retrieval. I'd have two to three jobs a month and most of them would be on the weekend. He would pay me a flat fee of ten grand a job—hazard pay because of the illegal nature of the job. If I got caught, I'd be on my own. That scared me. But not as much as what my future would look like if I couldn't stay in school.

All I wanted was to go to college so I could make a better life for myself. I worked so hard to get there, falling short and having to leave broke something in me. His offer came at precisely the time I couldn't refuse it.

For the first few months, the work was exciting, and lucrative, and I'd proven to be very good at slipping in and out of mansions and skyscrapers without being seen. I could do two jobs in a week if geography allowed and I was doing six or seven retrievals a month.

I not only paid my tuition, but I saved enough money to pay it for the next year, too. I finally had enough money to pay off the enormous credit debt my brother racked up in my name.

By the end of my junior year, I had money in the bank and had paid off the balance on the home equity loan my parents took out on their house.

I could have stopped but I didn't want to. Not yet.

I had a new goal in sight—law school. I ignored the irony of it and said yes when Michel asked me to spend the summer in France.

He had ten jobs lined up for the month. I told my family I had an internship for the summer and they believed me. Just like they had when I told them the money I earned came from my travel blog's advertising revenue.

I stayed in fabulous hotel rooms, ate amazing food, saw all the major landmarks. I should have been happy.

But I was having a hard time looking myself in the mirror. Worry about the immorality of what I was doing started to keep me up on the night. Lying to family and friends every single time we spoke had worn thin and I started avoiding their calls.

On the fourth job of the summer, on a balmy night in Nice, all that niggling doubt and guilt proved to be portent.

My life flashed before my eyes when the target's twelve-year-old grandson walked in on me as I was opening the safe and turned on the lights before I even realized he was there.

Panicked, I abandoned the job, climbed out of the window I'd pried open to enter the room and scaled the trellis as quickly as I could.

As I sprinted through the narrow streets, I prayed that the child hadn't gotten a good look at my face. I spent the next day scouring the papers and online media for reports of the break-in and sending Michel's calls to voicemails. After a couple of days, I felt comfortable leaving my flat to go to the airport.

I called Michel on my way there and quit.

I was doing this to pay for law school but what good would a law degree do me if I was arrested and tried for grand larceny?

His "you'll be back" barb fell on deaf ears. The relief I felt as soon as I told him I was done told me I'd made the right decision.

I met Evan in the airport lounge on my way home. We were reading the same book, *The Power of Myth* and started a conversation that lasted until we boarded our flight for Houston. He was in first class, I was flying economy and at the gate, he upgraded my seat so we could keep talking.

He was forty-five and I had just turned twenty-one, but I liked him. When he turned out to be a self-made mega millionaire who wanted to make me a pillow princess and take care of me so I could spend my senior year studying and applying to law school, I thought I'd finally found the answer to my prayers.

He set me up in an apartment off campus and came to see me there every weekend.

It was a dream…until it turned into a nightmare.

The day after that last fight, I swallowed my pride and called Michel.

"Cassie!"

I turn in the direction my name was called from with a ready smile. Michel strides into the crosswalk toward me. I haven't seen him since the day he came to my dorm room. I have no idea where he lives. We communicate by email and he wires my pay directly to my bank account. Dressed in a black suit that's got to feel like an oven in this heat, but there isn't a speck of sweat on his clean shaved bald head or face.

"Michel, hi!" My eyes drop to the telltale bulge of his jacket and my heart thuds against my chest. My gaze shoot back to his. "Why are you carrying?"

He adjusts his stance, tugs at the lapel of his blazer and gives me a thin-lipped smile. "Keep your voice down." His gaze darts past me and sweeps the crowded passenger pick-up area. "I'm head of the target's security detail. Have been for a few months and I like it. So don't fuck this up for me."

I let out a slow whistle and raise my eyebrows. Talk about fox guarding the hen house. "You think he'll keep you on after he gets robbed under your watch?"

He grimaces. "You let me worry about that."

My eyes dart back to the bulge underneath his jacket. "Is the person you're protecting someone with active threats to his life?"

"He's a political VIP. The general threat around him is always high. Is there a problem?" His expression is unreadable but the irritated impatient energy coming from him isn't.

"No problem at all." I give him a thumbs up for good measure. I'm lucky he brought me on to this job. I think he's an asshole but I don't want to get off on the wrong foot with him. "I was just trying to get the lay of the land."

He scoffs. "If I don't tell it to you, you don't need to know it. Okay?"

"Okay." I give him a two-finger salute.

He frowns and cups my elbow. "Come on. I'm taking you to the ferry."

I let him guide me through the parking garage and climb into his car without saying another word.

I'm buzzing for the details and a little sick to my stomach at the unexpected danger it now poses. I've done enough of these jobs to know that even elite security guards don't carry weapons they don't anticipate using.

"This is how it's going to go." Michel launches in without any small talk.

"You're going to be part of the hospitality staff at a small, privately owned resort. You'll do whatever the head of staff asks, wear the uniforms, sleep where you're told, and blend in. There's a private residence on the left lawn of the resort. It's a villa, two stories and occupied by the target and his personal staff. The ring you're here to retrieve is in a safe inside one of the bedrooms." He holds out his phone. "Here's a picture of it."

It is a gold signet ring inlaid with a black onyx star on the flat top of it.

"It's kept in a safe in one of the two bedrooms in the yellow corridor of the second floor."

It's pretty unremarkable. I'm no expert, but there's no way that ring is worth more than the hundred and fifty grand they're paying me to steal it. I know better than to say that, though. Rich people and their weird kinks are one thing I'll never understand.

"Does he ever wear it?"

"That doesn't matter." Michel mutters.

"Of course it does. If he wears it, I need to know so I—"

"Stop." He hisses and cuts his eyes at me. "Like I said, if you need to know, I'll tell you. The ring is in a safe," he snaps.

I bite back the other questions on my tongue. "Okay."

"The house alarm is only engaged overnight. However, there are security cameras that record twenty-four hours a day. In your capacity as waitstaff, you'll only have access to the house twice a day when you go in to deliver meals. As I said, the safe is one of three bedrooms."

"You said one of *two* bedrooms," I interject.

"And that's what I said just now, two." He holds up two fingers as I need the visual.

I heard what I heard but I'm not going to argue with him. "Check the unoccupied one first. If you don't find it there, you'll have to find a way into the bedroom of the target. By whatever means necessary."

I nod even though there are some things, no matter how necessary, I won't do. "Who is the target?"

"It doesn't matter. You aren't to ask any questions about him. Not that the staff could tell you much. And we all refer to him by his security detail code name, Wild Card."

I nod. "Got it. Are you going to show me a picture of him?"

"No. Just don't speak to anyone who isn't staying in the staff quarters with you. When you're in the private residence, you are to keep your eyes down, your mouth shut, and blend in."

"Okay."

"Besides retrieving this ring, your job is to be as benign as possible. So that if anyone catches you in the house, they'll believe whatever cover story you use."

"Right. Be benign as opposed to malignant," I quip.

"You have a week to get the ring, smart ass," he grumbles. "As soon as you hand it over, I'll wire you the money, take you the airport, and you'll be done."

He pulls to a full stop and throws the car into park. "We're here. When you get to the island, go straight to the resort, ask for Ama."

"Ama. Got it."

"She works for the target, does not know you are not really waitstaff. I'll be there working and keeping an eye on your flaky ass."

"I'm not flaky. I almost got caught. What did you want me to do?"

He grunts. "Don't make me regret giving you this chance. Get out."

He doesn't have to tell me twice.

* * * *

"Welcome aboard," the ferry driver greets me as I step on board. I am enthralled by the stunning beauty around me. I've never seen water so clear in my life.

Without Michel breathing down my neck, I can enjoy nature's display of its complexity and diversity. On the hour-long trip, we glide past a few small islands that the driver notes over the loudspeaker.

The Seychelles is one of those places I've used as a screensaver on my computer but never imagined I'd ever see. I'm breathless at the wonder of it. As beautiful as it is, I can't enjoy it.

I hope one day I can come back without the mantle of trespasser and thief around my neck. "We're approaching La Digue, the most beautiful island in Seychelles. Check your seats to make sure you take all your personal items with you. Welcome to paradise. Enjoy your stay."

Michel's instructions were clear. I'm to take an Uber to the resort and report to a person named Ama for my uniform, lodging and assignments.

I take in a deep, fortifying breath and take my time walking up the pier to the taxi stand. I turn to catch one last glimpse of the water, walking backwards as I take out my phone and capture the remarkable view. *How bad can it be if I'm looking at this all week?*

I drop my phone into my pocket and grab my suitcase's handle to turn around. "Hey, watch—" I hear him too late and crash into the man trying to warn me with a thud that knocks the wind out of me and pushes me back onto my heels. I windmill my arms to try and correct my balance but cry out as it proves in vain and my body teeters backward. I brace myself for a fall.

Instead, an arm wraps around my waist and I find myself staring into the mirrored lenses of a dark pair of Ray-Bans.

Even with his eyes hidden and his face covered in sweat, he's easily one of the most handsome men I've ever seen in person. He's got a mouth most women would envy and a nose that belongs in a museum. His pores are amazing. *I need to find out what he uses on his skin.*

"Are you alright?" he asks, still hovering over me, still holding me up as if I weighed nothing.

"Yes." I cough to clear the husk from my voice. "I'm sorry I wasn't watching where I was going."

"I was," he murmurs.

"You were...watching where I was going?"

"No. Where I was going. So, I saw you. Caught you." The heat from his hand seeps through the thin fabric of my sundress.

I can't see his eyes but I swear I can feel them on my face and I don't like that I can't see him.

And that's my cue to end this little...whatever it is.

"Can you let me up?" I press my hands to his chest.

"Oh." He starts as if he didn't realize he was holding me. "Yes, sorry." He straightens and lets me go. But the heat from his touch doesn't.

"Thanks for breaking my fall. I'm Cassie." I give a lame wave.

He flashes an unfairly perfect grin. "Nice to meet you. How long are you here?"

"All week. I'm working at the resort. You?" I ask as he starts to jog in place and glances at his watch.

"Two weeks. At least. So...maybe I'll see you around?"

"Sure. What's your name?"

"They call me Wild Card." He winks and runs off.

Oh shit. I've already fucked up. Well at least I know who to avoid.

I glance over my shoulder and watch him run away, his back muscles a thing of art and perfection, and sigh. "What a waste."

2

Failure

CASSIE

6 days later

"Wish you were here." I smile into the camera and turn a full circle to capture the stunning view behind me.

I close my eyes against the sun bathing my face and neck and tip my head back into the breeze and wish that all is as well as it appears.

But that six-second glimpse of tranquility I'm sending to my parents is a smoke screen. The raw beauty I'm surrounded by has become, in the course of the last week, a backdrop for my abysmal failure and fits of blind panic.

All I've managed to do in the last six days is serve drinks, deliver meals and collect enough tip money to pay my rent for three months. I'm not thrilled to be dressed like a pinup and subjected to the ogling eyes of my customers. But the perfect mix of sunshine and a seemingly perpetual breeze that sweeps up the hill from the sea is a constant reminder that I'm in paradise.

There have been a few moments where I've been able to forget that my survival, my future, all of it, depends on the one thing I can't seem to do. I've gone to bed every night hoping that tomorrow will be better. So far hope has gotten me nowhere.

Unless I get lucky and find a way to get that ring tonight, I'm going to leave here with nothing but these tips…the thought makes my stomach lurch dangerously.

How will I pay for law school? I paid off that debt but my credit won't be good enough to qualify for the private loans I'll need to pay my way. I could ask Evan for a loan...I shudder at giving him that kind of power over me.

But the thought of moving back home with my parents is unbearable. My parents scoffed at my pursuit of higher education. Who did I think I was thinking I could be a lawyer? Wanting to live in the "fancy" Rivers Wilde area instead of their working-class neighborhood that flooded every hurricane season.

Their attempts to shame and guilt me into staying where they could see me failed.

I wanted more and I was *so* close to having it.

"*There* you are." My coworker, Abby, steps into the little cover of bushes where I'm sitting. "I'm sorry the other servers are giving you shit. I don't know who started the rumor about you and Michel." She kicks off her black stilettos and joins me on the bench I thought was tucked out of plain sight.

I stifle a sigh of irritation. I came out here to be alone. But she's the only one of the staff who's even spoken to me this week. The least I can do is be nice. I scoot over to give her more room to sit. "I'm only here for a week, who cares what they think."

She nudges my shoulder. "Are *sure* you okay?"

I cast her a quick smile and turn my eyes back to the sea. "I'm fine. Look around me, how could I not be."

"I mean, if you *are* sleeping with Michel, who could blame you?"

I don't know if she's fishing for information or being sincere. "I'm *not* sleeping with him. If I was, it wouldn't be anyone's business. I don't know why they even care. I wouldn't."

She giggles and nudges me again. "They're just jealous because he's paid so much attention to you."

"I hadn't noticed." Of course I have. I shudder at the memory of Michel's eyes on me. He's watched me like a hawk, interrogated me every chance he's gotten. "He's gross, Abby. He's only watching me because he doesn't want me to fuck up. If they want him, let them know they can have him."

She giggles. "I like how you say it straight."

I sigh. "Life is too short for anything else. My grandpa used to say I didn't talk a lot, but when I did, I made the oxygen count." I laugh to myself at the memory of those conversations.

My heart gives a squeeze. And even though I'll never get over him being gone, I'm glad that even though I'm so far from the girl I was when he died, I can still hear his voice.

Her eyes narrow. "You know...there aren't many of us from the States with the security clearance and connections to work at properties like this. I thought I knew everyone. Where'd you come from?"

My preparation kicks in seamlessly. "I'm a student. This is only my second international job."

Her eyes go wide. "Oh...and you scored a major one, too. You must have *some* connections."

I shake my head and force a smile. "I'm telling you. I don't know how that happened. It's just luck." I almost choke on the lie.

Luck has never been kind to me.

I've *always* had to force its hand.

"So...how *do* you know Michel?" she asks.

The cover story we created rolls off my tongue with ease. "I met him last summer. I was bumming around in France, working and eating and making friends."

"That sounds like fun." She kicks the pebbled gravel.

"It is." *Or would have been.*

"Break's over." I get to my feet and slip my shoes back on, smoothing my hair down. "Nice chatting."

I walk away before she can reply and hurry down the hall and out to the other side of the house where a massive tent has been set up.

"Do you think he'd let me serve in the main house if I asked to?" Abby catches up to me.

I press my lips together and stop short. "I didn't ask him if I could stay. Those were the terms of my employment. I wish I could help."

I stride away and her hurried steps clatter against the pavement like spilling marbles. I stop to check my appearance in the mirrored wall that lines the long corridor back to the lobby of the resort. The reverb of my stout, solid heel hitting the travertine tile floors is a reminder of how many ways I was set up to fail at this job.

Even barefoot, footfalls are impossible to mask.

I use one of the linen napkins in the pearl and gold lined tissue box on the table below the mirror and dab the shine away from my nose.

Abby appears next to me again. Her warm smile is gone. "Whatever. You don't want to share the wealth...that's fine. I don't blame you. And honestly, I'm saving myself for the big prize tomorrow."

"What's that?"

"The Wild Card. Lord of the Manor. I hear he owns all of this." She waves a hand around her. "I've heard he's hot. I know he's rich. And from what I hear, he's not an asshole. A man like him can change your life with the snap of his fingers."

"Sounds like a unicorn. Are you sure he's real?" I quip, unsure why I'm trying to throw her off his scent.

"No one's seen him all week. But I know he's here and if I find him, I'm going to make my move."

I'm shocked by the urge I have to claw her eyes out. "Good luck with that."

I give her a tight smile and head back inside.

As soon as I do, I wish I hadn't.

Michel is there waving me over before he slips out the doors leading from the back of the house to the pool.

There's no point trying to evade him. I take my time following him and think of the best way to save myself. I make a silent promise to the universe that if I get out of this in one piece this will be the last time I do one of these jobs.

I've tried all week, but I haven't found a way into the private residence of the house. I carry The Wild Card's meals into a tiny terraced verandah with an ocean view on the first floor. The stairway up to the bedrooms has cameras trained on it at all times. I haven't had a chance.

I step outside and Michel is standing by the pool. "Come over here, Cassie."

I'd rather not, but he's running the show.

I grit my teeth and smile as I approach him.

"I've been watching you," he says with a gaze that I *think* is supposed to intimidate me.

"It's a free country and I've got a nice ass. I don't blame you," I joke.

He doesn't crack a smile. "You've got one more day."

I smile with a nonchalance I don't feel. "That's all I need."

His eyes narrow. "If you can't do it, just say so now. We'll get someone else."

I scoff. "If someone else was capable of doing the job, you wouldn't have called me in the first place."

His scowl intensifies. "You're right about that. You are unreliable and flighty. And one more day isn't going to change that. You failed."

"The stairs are guarded all day. I need more time."

"Yes, I'm aware of the extenuating circumstances. I can convince my boss to give you more time."

I sag with relief. "Thank you."

"But first," he holds up a finger. "I'll need a little incentive. The kind you give on your knees." He leers at me and I recoil.

I curl my lip in disgust. "That wasn't part of the deal."

This isn't the first time I've been propositioned or had my job held over my head in exchange for parts of me that I would never give to a man like him. Or anyone who felt they could demand it of me.

"If you want to leave here with anything, you don't have any other choice."

I grit my teeth. "In your dreams. I've always got a choice."

3

Pressure

Leo

The small, private peninsula on the island of La Digue where my father built the smallest hotel in his portfolio and his personal retreat is twelve miles in circumference. The sun's setting fast, but the light is holding and I'm determined to get this run in.

A week cooped up recovering from whatever bug I caught on my flight over is not how I planned to spend my time here. I'm just glad I'm well enough to get outside and blow off the cobwebs from being in bed for so long.

The weather has been outstanding and I breathe deep as I start to settle into a rhythm.

I love my morning run in Central Park for its diversity and community. Depending on where I enter, the landscape and architecture can vary wildly. Every day was different.

I was worried that the monotony of the seemingly endless beach, rock formations and trees would make it even harder to push through this first attempt. But I was wrong. The walking trails my father created are made of the same soil that grounds and nourishes the massive mango trees lining the paved paths that the golf carts use.

The give of it under my feet puts a spring in my step. The sea salt, flowers, and fertile earth fill the air with smells that tell a different story with each breath. They are an elixir to my weakened muscles and my recovering lungs.

I forgot how much I love it here. There's no place on Earth that feels closer to true nature than Seychelles.

The resort and home that are nestled into the lush beaches of the peninsula were designed to look like part of the landscape.

The resort rises up out of the foliage like a temple.

The villa's foundation is carved from the rock of the cliff it sits atop like a beacon.

My father loved this place more than any other. It was called the Eastern Castle because he spent so much time here.

His career and life required him to entertain frequently. So, he built the lodge like a hotel because he couldn't abide anyone staying in his home. In more recent years, it's been converted into a commercial resort that anyone with deep enough pockets can book a stay in.

A die-hard James Bond fan, the impressive seventy-thousand-square-foot guest house was inspired by the home in *For Your Eyes Only*. The fifty acres of lush, naturally beautiful beach and forest are a testament to my father's power and wealth.

He designed and paid for every square inch of the paradise built on what had been an uninhabited no-man's-land.

I don't understand why he left it, and so many of his other favorite things, to the child he never even publicly acknowledged.

A week of bed rest has taken its toll and by the time I round the bend of Ring Road, the island's main artery, I'm fighting for each breath. But I keep going.

I need to get back into fighting shape and make sure the diplomatic dinner I'm hosting goes off without a hitch.

Stepping into my father's shoes has created a crushing case of imposter syndrome. If I can prove to my stepmother that I can be useful, maybe she'll stop being ashamed of my existence. Allow me to be his son now that he's gone.

I thought being here—where he and my mother had been so happy—would make me feel closer to him. I'd planned to get to know the staff I'd inherited, but a week of being cooped up in my room made that impossible.

Now, I wave to a man dressed in khaki green, pruning a hedge, and say hi. He quickly averts his gaze to the camellia as if it's suddenly sprouted a pineapple.

I sigh. This was my father's place.

These are still his people.

I wish my brother had come and I wasn't alone hosting the dinner next Saturday.

"Assistant, call Biz."

My brother answers on the first ring. ""Leo, how be?"

"All good. Just want—"

"Hold a minute." He speaks to someone in a muffled tone.

His use of Pidgin English when he answered the phone is something he would never have done if my father was alive.

Of all my father's children, Bismark is the only one who has ever treated me like a brother. But he looks and sounds so much like our father, and followed his footsteps into politics, I always assumed he wanted the life my father was grooming him for. But now…I wonder if he ever had a choice.

"Sorry about that Leo, what's up?" He comes back on the line as abruptly as he answered it.

"Just wanted to tell you that all our expected guests have arrived and are comfortably ensconced in their day of spa treatments. Everything is ready for next week."

"Excellent. Thank you for doing this for us."

I note his use of the *us* as a reminder that I am not one of them—the children who are allowed to call him father in public. I know Biz didn't mean to remind me, so I don't let my discomfort show. "It's my pleasure. I'm just glad I'm feeling better."

"Were you really sick? I thought you just wanted to avoid the festivities."

"I was sick. But at least now you know, for the next time, that the hotel staff is perfectly capable of playing host."

"Well, the dinner next week will be very different. It's a diplomatic event."

"Everything's ready."

"And what about…what's her name? Fendi?"

"Chanel. And she cancelled when I told her she'd need to submit to a background check to attend."

"Stop letting your American friends set you up with women who can't fathom the life you have to live. Next time, listen to your older brother."

"There won't be a next time. I'm done being set up at all. The women either balk at the background check or want me to submit to one, attest to the health of my sperm count, and meet with their estate planning attorney before the first date. There's no happy medium. I'm just going to let life happen as it will."

He laughs, but it's brusque, dismissive, familiar and disconcerting. "Spoken like a real Yank. Don't learn this lesson the hard way, Leo. You can't let life *happen*. Not when you're…you."

His words twist and sour my gut at the reminder of everything I've designed my life to forget. "I've got to go, Biz. Make sure they confiscate the phones of everyone at your table. Call me next time you're in New York. It would be nice to see you."

"Try to enjoy the party, Leo"

As if I could when everyone thinks my father is my uncle.

Revealing my true identity is something my stepmother would die before she allowed.

But she's allowed me access and contact I've never had before. I got to join the rest of them during the official ceremonies for my father's funeral.

And this dinner I'm hosting on their behalf is my first official function. The pressure for it to go off without a hitch is immense.

As I round the bend to my house, gearing up for one more lap, loud voices ring out from over the gate that runs along the back of the property.

I stop, surprised to hear raised voices coming from the resort. I've heard nothing but gaiety and laughter since I've been here.

I stop, catching my breath and letting the ocean breeze cool my overheated, throbbing body and listen.

"I said I won't do it." A woman's voice reverberates and the American accent piques my curiosity. I turn and start up the path that leads to the back of the house.

"And I said that if you want to get paid, you have to play by my rules." The even louder response, from a rumbling male voice accented with the jambalaya of the Seychellois takes me from curiosity to irritation.

I turn down the wide, open avenues that connect the separate living spaces of the house together and lead to the resort's pool.

A woman, petite and scantily clad in a ridiculously short maid's uniform, her hair scraped back into a bun, has her back to me and stands between the man and the pool.

Her arms are gripped by the massive hands of the head of security, Michel. He's got a foot of height on her and is built like a professional body builder.

This guy is tall enough that my 6' 2" frame would be looking up at him, too.

She yanks herself free and whirls around, stalking around the pool and in my direction. As she gets closer, her face comes into view like a bolt of lightning.

Her.

I should have known.

When I bumped into her that day, I was struck speechless.

She's beautiful, to be sure. But it was her energy— the same unbridled and tightly contained energy that hurricanes have— that kept my attention.

The view from my verandah allows me to observe the entirety of the hotel's leisure areas. It wasn't the worst consolation prize I've been handed. I got to watch her work all week. Work is meant only in the loosest of terms. She's spilled countless drinks, brought several guests the wrong order, and spent more time chatting with guests than actually serving them.

There's a sort of chaotic joy in everything she does. Watching her while I eat has been an unexpectedly entertaining way to pass my time. The only thing I lamented more than missing my runs was not getting to follow up on that first encounter.

Even though I've seen her at least a dozen times, I'm struck by how *interesting* her face is.

I wouldn't call her pretty—her eyes too narrow in contrast to the boldness of her cheekbones, her voluptuous mouth, her prominent broad nose, her high sloping forehead.

She reminds me of the stunningly beautiful Xhosa women I met during my summer in Cape Town. Yet, the elegance in those women's demeanor is entirely absent from hers.

And when she whips around to face her aggressor, her eyes flash, her lips pucker and her nostrils flare.

Her anger is as impressive as her joy.

A sliver of sympathy slips past my annoyance at the man she's now got in her sights.

"Don't you ever put a hand on me, you clown," she snarls up at him.

The height disparity between them is comical.

"A clown who just fired you."

"Exactly," she smirks.

My shoulders shake with my stifled chuckle. *I like her spirit.*

"Bitch," Michel growls. And with a shove at her shoulder, he sends her flying into the water.

4

Hero

LEO

She surfaces with a gasp and flails for a second before she finds her balance in the water and glares at Michel. I watch for a second to make sure she can swim.

The bird's-eye view I've enjoyed all week is about to come to an end.

But it might not be so bad being up close and personal with Ms. Chaos. I step out from the shelter of the hedge.

"What's going on here?"

Michel freezes. His expression goes from irritated and fierce to relaxed and subordinate. He steps in front of her, blocking her from my sight. "Sir, nothing. I'm sorry about the noise. I've got this under control and this employee has been terminated."

"How long have you worked for this family?" I cross my arms over my chest and let my displeasure show on every inch of my face.

"A year." He speaks through gritted teeth.

"And did you read your contract before you signed it?"

He blinks in confusion. "Yes, sir."

"Then have you forgotten the clause about workplace behavior? We have a zero tolerance policy when it comes to employee conduct."

His already ruddy cheeks redden. His chin twitches, but he keeps his expression passive. "But sir—she's not an employee, she's a temp."

"I'm not talking about her conduct, I'm talking about yours."

"I quit," she shouts from the middle of the pool.

I look over my shoulder and see her doggy paddling slowly toward the steps. "Are you okay?"

"Better than he's going to be when I get out of here," she shouts. Her voice is remarkably clear, her eyes are locked on Michel.

I turn my attention back to him.

I'm more than ready to get rid of this buffoon.

I was told he was a real asset and an experienced personal security professional. But he's always had a hard time meeting my eye. It was my first red flag that he wasn't right to be head of security.

Watching him this week has only reinforced that feeling.

He treats the staff like they're cattle when he thinks no one is watching.

As I approach the pair, I send a quick text to my assistants and ask them to gather the staff in an hour.

It's time I let Michel know that the order of things here has changed.

"You're fired."

His eyes narrow like he can't believe what he's just heard. "No, but she—"

"I'm not interested." Irritated, I sigh. I don't know how Biz hires his people, but for this weekend at least, this man works for me and I don't want him here.

"Go see Ama. She'll cut you a check and help you make arrangements to get home."

"You can't fire me—"

"Actually, I can. I have. Thank you for your service."

I dismiss him without another word and turn back to the woman climbing out of the pool.

I hold my hand out. "Here, let me."

"What?" Her head snaps up and she quirks her brow at my hand. "Oh. Thank you."

She links her fingers with mine and her slick skin is cool against my overheated hand. The touch is electric.

Our eyes meet and hold as she climbs out.

Water pours from her uniform. She yanks the shirt tail out from her skirt's waistband, unbuttons it and peels it off her body. I almost swallow my tongue.

She's wearing a very modest sports bra but it does wonders for her. She tosses the shirt to the ground like it's a snake.

"Thank you," she breathes out, gathering her braids and twisting them to wring the water out.

I grab a towel from the stand next to the cabana beside me and hand it over with my eyes averted.

"You can look now."

She's wrapped the towel around herself. "I'm sorry that happened."

She gives me a once-over and sighs. "Thank you."

"I fired him. Go see Ama and she'll get you something to wear and sort you out."

"Okay, sure. Thanks." She gives a tight smile, turns on her heel, and speeds away.

"I press the button on my earbud. "Assistant, call Ama."

I head back to my room while Ama's phone rings. She picks up, out of breath. "Leo, what's wrong?"

I snort. "Why do you think something's wrong?"

"Because *today*, everything is wrong. And I don't want to rush you, but I'm putting out three fires right now. Next time you decide to host an event in another country, don't."

I laugh and relax. "There'll be no next time, so don't worry."

"It would have been better if we'd been able to bring in our own security. These goons your brother hired make me nervous. He hates me and they look at me like they know it."

I sigh. "I don't know why you think my brother has a problem with you."

"Ummmm, because he does. He's asked you to fire me more than once."

I have a large staff, a complex schedule and travel that is a logistical nightmare. And because of Ama, my long-term personal assistant, my life stays in order while I live it. She hires everyone I need when I need them, and all I have to do is make sure everyone's paycheck is signed or their direct deposit is sent.

Ama handles it all so seamlessly, I forget I have more than two employees. But in the two weeks we've been in the Seychelles, she's been frazzled and stressed every time we've spoken.

"I'm glad you called because I do need to tell you something. Mona and Eli are here."

I stop in my tracks and hit the camera button.

Her face pops on my screen and she holds a hand up. "First, let me say I'm sorry."

I ignore her pointless apology. "How did *that* sneak up on us?"

She winces. "I don't know. I really don't."

"They didn't even RSVP."

"But they're here. I saw them get into a car at arrivals. Together." She whispers the last word of her sentence.

Dread pools in my stomach. None of this is good. "Shit."

"Who knows? Maybe she's not here for—"

"What else could she be here for, Ama?" I close my eyes so I can focus on creating the sequence of events I need to put into motion. I open my eyes as it starts to fall into place. "First, find out where she's staying."

She pulls out her phone. "They're staying at the guest house."

"Here? How could you have missed that?"

"I swear I didn't. They didn't give any notice. I would have known."

"Make sure there's a welcome basket sent over." I pace back and forth. "Also, call the stylist and tell her we need her after all."

There's a beat of silence and I glance at the phone to make sure the call didn't drop out. "Hello?"

"Oh...Is Chanel coming after all?"

"No." I stifle my sigh of irritation.

"Then why do we need her?"

"Ama, everyone here reports to you. Except for me. Just do it, please."

"It's already done. I only paused because you are such a stickler about managing expenses. I'm surprised you'd pay for something you no longer have a use for."

"Oh, I have use for it. I've found a date for tonight."

"Okay. Do they have the security clearance?"

"Yes. She's been here all week."

"Who?"

"The young woman who's coming to see you. She was fired by Michel. Who I have also fired."

"You did? Why?"

"He pushed the woman into the pool."

"God, he's terrible. So, do you want me to restore her position?"

"No. But make sure she doesn't leave the island until I have a chance to talk to her again."

"Okay. But Leo, why?" I can picture her pushing her glasses up her nose and squaring her shoulders.

"I've got plans for her."

5

The way we live.

CASSIE

"What a waste of time." I stand and snatch the plastic bag full of my wet clothes off the floor.

"I'm sorry you feel that way." Ama, a petite, pretty brown-skinned woman folds her hands primly on the desk in front of her and smiles as if she's not playing with my life. "But as I told you, I can't cut your check before I clear it with my boss. I'll need until close of business."

"And what am I supposed to do for a day?"

She hands me an envelope. "You will be allowed to remain in your room and have access to staff dining for another day."

"But I'm still fired?" I demand, my arms crossed.

"Yes. Unfortunately. I wasn't instructed to reverse Michel's decision. But as I said, give me a day and we'll make sure you get your pay."

"I don't have a day."

She cocks her head to the side and narrows her eyes at me. "According to your contract, you do. Your last official day was tomorrow. Has something changed?"

I flush under her stare and tamp down my panic. "No. I just—I want to get out of here."

"And you will." Her phone rings and she purses her lips, holds up a finger and answers it.

Her calm and collected demeanor fades to irritation as she listens to whoever is on the other line. "How? Ask him to come see me. Tell him to hurry, security was supposed to be on this." She sighs and drops her forehead into her hand. "I should have known not to trust that Michel. I want you to confirm that he actually left the island right away."

Fear licks at my insides and wakes me up.

I'm *very* far from home and the last thing I need is to make someone suspicious enough to start poking into the fake background they created for me. The person who brought me here got fired because of me and is unaccounted for.

I know he's not gone because he's still after the ring. My cut is a fraction of his, there's no way he'll abandon the job. For all I know has already found someone to replace me with.

Frustration makes my eyes burn with unshed tears. This is so unfair. There wasn't a wall I could scale to reach the bedrooms. The only way up was up the stairs. And with those cameras recording I didn't dare chance it.

If my only choices are being broke or risking jail, I'd rather be broke.

Any day.

A man bursts into the room. "It's *all* the cameras. The main power to them died. We can't get anyone here to look at it until—."

Ama clears her throat. "Thank you for the update."

The man glance at me and his eyes go wide. "Oh. Sorry, Ama. I didn't realize someone else was here."

"It's fine. She's leaving." She fixes her smile and looks back at me.

I wasn't done, but it's obvious she is. "Thank you." *For nothing.*

As if she heard my unspoken words, her smile turns sardonic. "You're *very* welcome. I'll send someone to the staff quarters to collect the clothes I lent you."

I look down at the worn khaki shorts and the t-shirt, both two sizes too small for me. "I'll have them ready." Inside I'm equal parts livid at myself and the assholes I'm stuck on this island with.

But I smile as I leave, don't slam the door shut behind me. Once I'm safe, eighteen-year-old me would be proud. I keep my composure. When I'm home, I can let myself stew, but I check my watch and groan. It's not even noon. I wonder if he's back from his run yet and how long I'll have to wait to get my money.

The cameras are out.

I stop pacing. Oh my God. He's not here. The cameras are down.

This is my chance.

Even if Michel *has* found someone else, the likelihood that they'll arrive today is slim. I could take the ring, catch the ferry to get to the airport, and be home free in a couple of hours. I smile as I imagine Michel's reaction when I call him to say I have the ring.

I make a beeline toward the palm tree lined path that connects the resort to the house. The offices are located on the eastern side of the property, closer to the private residence than any other part of the estate.

The first set of doors I encounter is always how I enter a house. Even if it's farthest away from my destination, it's the safest way in and the quickest way out.

I test the doors. They're locked. But only barely. I pull the small tool I keep clipped inside my bra out with my fingers and maneuver it into place on reflex. I've been picking locks since I was eleven years old and a latchkey kid.

It's been a while since I've found one challenging, but I'm surprised how flimsy this one is. Why have security on the inside if you don't protect the outside?

This is my job, but there's a thrill in being where I'm not supposed to be that I get every single time. The tiny click of the lock disengaging excites me.

The house is dark, the only light from the moon as it pours in through the glass panes of the doors and windows that line the library I've entered.

Regret taps me on the shoulder as I hurry past the shelves of books and out into the hallway. I know this space because I've walked it, but in the dark there's something sinister about it.

Or maybe it's because *I'm* here for sinister reasons.

I walk down the hall to the second set of stairs that start at the end of the second floor.

Unlike the straight staircase that leads from the first to the second floor, this one wraps around each floor's landing. The steps are the same white gleaming blond wood that lines the first flight but a colorful array of light dances over them from above.

I lean over the sleek wrought-iron and wood rail and peer up.

"Oh my God." The ceiling in the center of the void made by the stairs is a stunning beautiful stained-glass mural. It's nestled into a circular cut-out in the white stucco ceiling. I recognize the pattern is inspired by the flag of Seychelles. The glorious display isn't visible from the first floor.

As I start my ascent, I get the sense that I'm entering a space that is sacred. This part of the property is only for the family and the people they trust enough to let into their private quarters. the part of the house where they actually live.

I swallow down the ball of nerves. This is the break I've been waiting for all week.

"Shake it off, Gold. This is perfect." I inhale a deep breath and then let it out to expel some of the anxiety buzzing around in my chest.

I open the door to the first room on the long yellow walled corridor. I step inside, flip the switch to turn on the lights and gasp. The room is huge, tranquil and bright. A bed, bigger than any I've ever seen takes up almost an entire wall.

It faces a floor-to-ceiling window that opens out to a view of the ocean and a beach of sand so white it seems supernatural. The water is a crystal-clear blue and on either side of the beach are rock formations that form a small cove and are nestled in lush vegetation that's bursting with bright voluptuous blooms.

"What are you doing in there?"

The six words I dread more than any other nearly stop my heart. I freeze mid-step and wrack my brain for a story that might save me from this incredibly perilous cliff edge.

"It's impossible that you didn't hear me. So I'm going to assume you haven't given me an answer because you don't have one." Wild Card's voice has the same edge it did when he spoke to Michel by the pool.

Fuck.

I spin on my heel and bite down on the tip my tongue hard to pull a believable sob out of me.

I cover my mouth with my hand and keep my eyes on the ground. "I'm sorry. I thought this room was vacant."

"It is. But this part of the house isn't open to anyone but the family and our personal staff."

Shit. "I-I'm sorry. I didn't know. I wanted to change before I went to see Ama, and I have no idea where Michel might be lurking. I wasn't sure if I'd be safe using the staff facilities so I came here."

I cast my tear damp eyes up with a pleading expression and hope that there's a chink in that unimpressed and impatient demeanor of his where some compassion might find purchase.

I look up into the eyes of the man who holds my future in his hands.

His expression is tight with irritation and he shoves his hands in his pockets and rocks back on his heels. "Why? Has something happened? Did he bother you again?"

I drop my eyes, cover my face with my hands, and think feverishly for a way out of this disaster. "I hated working for him."

"So why the tears?"

I jerk my head back and give him a critical once-over. "Because he hired me and left without paying me. Your lady says I'm not on the payroll. So I came here for nothing. You don't understand…I take care of so many people. I need the money. And as shitty as he is, I wouldn't have complained if he hadn't crossed that line. Now I'm screwed." I hiss miserably.

"So, what now?" he asks.

"I don't know. I can't believe I let my temper get the best of me like that." I pout and wrap my arms around myself. "Now, I have no job, no place to stay until my flight out of here on Sunday, and the money I would have made, that made coming all the way here worth it, I won't earn. And honestly, I'm just…really tired." It's the truest thing I've said and the truest thing I feel. Real tears pool in my eyes and I let them. I need one moment of honesty in this mess.

I'm *so* tired of taking care of everyone but myself. Of being at other people's mercy. Of not having anyone take care of me. I cover my face and try to compose myself.

Fake crying is one thing, but crying for real is too pathetic.

I still have my pride.

"So…what are you going to do?"

I shrug and press my lips together in a grim smile. "I don't know. I was going to figure it out after I dried off and had a good, private cry."

He purses his lips and averts his gaze. His hand taps his chin. "How much would you have made if you'd worked the party?"

I wince at the reminder of how much money I'm leaving on the table if I have to leave sooner than I'd planned.

"The job posting said it paid two-hundred dollars an hour for the week with a five-thousand dollar bonus for tomorrow. So…" I pretend to do the math in my head and drop my shoulders. "I would have made fifteen k." I groan and shake my head to drive home the magnitude of my despair. "I *need* that money."

"Have a seat, Cassie…what's your last name?"

"Why?"

He nods, "Okay, Cassie Why, I think I can help you."

I bite back a bark of surprised laughter and frown at him "That's not my last name, but let's go with it. How can you help me?" I wipe my tear-streaked face and sit up a little straighter.

A tiny smile lifts the left side of his face and my mouth goes dry.

It's not right that he looks like that.

"I can make sure you leave here with double the money you would have."

My heart stutters but I narrow my eyes. "Again, *how?*"

"I'll give it to you."

That is the *very* last thing I expected him to say. I blink in surprise. "Why?"

"Because you're going to help me, too."

I cross my arms and purse my lips as I give him a frosty once-over. "If this is some sort of sexual proposition, don't waste your breath. The answer is no."

I'm desperate and he's cute. But... I'd rather face the consequences of failure than do *that*.

He rolls his shoulders and lets out a deep breath. "Rest assured Ms...Why, that is the last thing on my mind. No offense. But you're not really my type."

The floor falls out from underneath whatever was left of my vanity and I wish to God it would take me with it. "Okay. Sorry. It's just…it wouldn't have been the first time." I press my hands together and bow in apology. "Please go on."

His expression remains neutral as he nods and points to the sitting room. "Let's sit." He strides out without waiting and I can tell he's not used to anything but obedience. I want to make him say please just for the sake of manners.

But a few minutes ago, I was on cracking ice and royally fucked. And now…I might get out of here in one piece.

I follow him into the room and settle into a chair across from him. I cross my legs and shift my weight while he types away on his phone like he didn't just say he wanted to talk.

I want to tell him to hurry up and say whatever it is he wants, but I just sit on my hands and smile as blandly as I can.

Finally, he looks up at me, his expression even more guarded than it had been a moment prior. "I'm hosting a party here next weekend. My date had to cancel last minute and I want you to take her place."

I scoff and glare at him. "Didn't I *just* say I wouldn't do anything like that?"

He gives me a tight smile. "And didn't I just say you're not my type?"

"I heard you. Maybe type means something else to you than it does to me."

"I didn't ask you to sleep with me. I asked you to be my date to a black-tie diplomatic dinner at my home. I need you to sit next to me, be nice to my guests, and give me a reason to leave early."

I narrow my eyes at him. "And then?"

"You go home. I'll pay you the fifteen thousand dollars you were expecting, and double it."

It's not even half of my fee but it's a hell of a lot more than zero. "Wow. Okay. But I'll need a place to stay. The resort is the only place to stay on this island. The rooms there start at a grand a night."

He nods. "And it's unlikely, given the dignitaries staying there, that they'd even rent you a room."

"Well, I'm not staying in the staff quarters."

He shrugs. "You can stay here."

The offer makes my head spin. I came here to steal from him. And I may be doing him a favor, but he's saving my ass. In ways I don't deserve.

The twinge of guilt fades as I turn to face my unwitting savior.

He's nice, but it's easy to be generous when you're rich enough to have a house like this.

It wasn't until I started doing this work that I saw the opulent comfort and soothing cleanliness that the rich take for granted.

Most of us live with cobwebbed corners and dusty picture frames because who has time to clean when you're working, cooking, going to school, and trying to keep your family together?

The first time I walked into a house that was cleaned from top to bottom on a regular basis, I'd fallen in love at first sight with the sterile, safe, intentional cleanliness of it.

I wanted to live that way.

All my jobs have involved me joining the staff of one of these homes. Like here, the employees usually sleep in separate, less luxurious quarters. But even those were nicer than the nicest house I've ever lived in.

"Well?"

I blink up at him, my mind suddenly blank. "Well what?"

He sighs. "I've offered you a solution. Spend the rest of your time here as my guest. Be my date for a night. I'll pay you for your time and promise to give you a glowing reference." He's watching me and for the first time I see something more than equanimity in his face. His expression is urgent, his body poised as if against a blow.

Was he *nervous*?

I'd put money on it that he was. This matters to him.

"So...I can have my own room here this week?"

"Yes."

"There's one thing I want besides the pay..."

He shrugs again. "There's very little you could ask for that I can't afford."

"I want to not have to take care of anybody for a week. I want to eat food I didn't have to cook myself. And I want to wake up without an alarm clock. I want to catch up on my television shows."

He types something on his phone. "I can give you that for five days. The event is in seven, you'll need time to get ready."

I eye him skeptically. He's probably just saying whatever it'll take for me to say yes.

But the look in his eyes is sincere.

Either my bullshit meter is broken…or he's the real deal.

And this is all the good luck I've never known coming at once. He's a wild card for real.

"Okay. I'll do it."

He makes a show of sagging in relief. "Thank you, Cassie."

"How do you know my name?" I don't catch myself soon enough to stop surprise from showing on my face.

His eyebrows furrow. "You told me."

I shake my head. "You remembered?"

His slow smile lifts one corner of his sensual mouth. "You make quite a first impression. And now, I don't think I'll ever forget it."

If he hadn't told me I wasn't his type, I would have sworn it was desire sharpening his gaze and turning his voice rough. My body responds like it is and gooseflesh ripples up my arms.

"Please, call me Leo."

I take a step back and cross my arms over my chest to hide the effect the gravel of his voice has had on my nipples. "I… okay, Leo. Umm…I don't really have anything to wear to a black-tie event."

He glances at his watch. "There's a closet full of clothes upstairs you can go wild in. If you find something you like and need an alteration, I have a tailor and stylist who will be at your disposal whenever you're ready."

"Whose clothes are in this closet you want me to go wild in?"

He holds a finger up and presses it to his ear. "Is she back onboard?"

He nods at whatever the person on the other end of the line says, and gives me a thumbs ups. "Tell her to bring everything she was going to and to make sure there's plenty of blue to choose from."

Questions brim on my lips but I force myself to be quiet. I have stumbled onto something better than I could have dreamed.

"What's your shoes size, Cassie?"

"Seven and a half."

"Seven and half. No. I'll tell you later."

He presses his lips together as he listens to the person on the other line. "I know you'll make it happen. I have faith in you. See you tomorrow."

He hangs up and turns back to me.

I shake my head and frown at him. "Who was that on the phone?"

"Just making sure everything is ready once you've had your five days. Food is easy."

"Okay." I'm a little stunned at how efficiently he's managed the pretty major curveball I threw at him. Just like he managed Michel earlier.

A decisive, take-charge attitude is my kink. Who knew?

The universe hates me. I'm sure of it now. Why else would it show me exactly what I want after I've done things to ensure I'll never have it?

He casts a glance around the room. "Since you wandered into this room, you can have it for the duration of your stay. I'll have someone bring your things up from the staff house. My mother's room is the room directly across from yours. Her closet is on the right. Shoes are upstairs, dresses in the very back on the right. I'll be back." He strides away.

"Hey, where are you going?" I call after him, my mind racing to try and remember everything he's just said.

His phone is already at his ear.

"Hello?" I call.

He raises a hand and waves but doesn't turn back. And he disappears around the corner without answering my question.

Shit.

I walk into my bedroom and am struck again by its beauty. And my good fortune. I'm the proverbial wolf in sheep's clothing.

I walk to the closet. The safe is in here somewhere.

So actually... *not* shit.

6

Let me entertain you.

Cassie

There are twenty-three different types of bananas that grow in the Seychelles and this week, I've had a sample of nearly all of them. Today's might be my favorite—or maybe it's the coconut cream and sugar baked into them. I shove the last bite into my mouth and groan in pleasure.

Breakfast isn't the only decadent thing about my mornings as a guest in this magnificent house. This verandah is small but the view it offers of the grounds makes it feel like I'm sitting on the edge of a universe. I can see the whole resort from here.

But after three days of looking and not finding any sign of a safe, this little staycation of mine has lost some its shine. I haven't dared to roam beyond these corridors, but I've searched every room on it.

I've taken countless pictures but they pale in comparison to the view my naked eye affords. It's been fun to send them to my parents and friends and read their reactions. It would be nicer to experience it in person with someone.

I take a final gulp of coffee and lean back in my chair to think about how to avoid death by boredom.

I've enjoyed being a layabout…but the part of me that likes living with other people—even when they're annoying— is starting to regret asking to be left alone.

"How's your breakfast, Ms. Cassie?" The cook, Hannah, is the only constant face I've seen this week. She's chatty and warm and if it wasn't for her, I would have been lonelier than I might have been able to bear.

I give her a huge thumbs up.

"It's delicious. Thank you for going to the trouble."

"No trouble. That banana dish is Mr. Leo's favorite, I usually make it for dessert but he requested it to break his fast."

I sit up straight and put the toast I was about to shovel into my mouth down. "He's here?"

"Yes. You eat at the same time, so he's been taking meals in his room because he said you were to be alone."

My cold, cynical heart purrs at the way her words wrap around. Then they sink in. "He's been eating alone in his room?"

She laughs. "No need to look so worried, Ms. Cassie. There's a table in the kitchen, also. He eats in there with me in the evenings. He's fine, dear."

I fix my face, cursing how easy it is to read when I'm not careful. "Can you show me where he is now? I'd like to thank him for his hospitality."

I follow her down the hall, and then up another set of stairs I hadn't realized were there. We walk up four short steps and enter his private suite. The sympathy I was feeling for him not being able to enjoy the view in the dining room wanes a little. He's got a garden view instead of the ocean, but it's nothing to sneeze at.

"Mr. Leo?" she calls and crosses the room to knock on one of the three doors that line the wall.

"Come in." His voice is muffled through the wall but he sounds like he's just woken up.

She beckons me forward, "Go on."

"Is he in bed?" I ask, my eyes dart to the door and back to her.

She brushes my worry away. "He's up with the sun. I brought his breakfast in before I brought yours."

I wait until she closes the door to his suite behind her before I go into his room. He's sitting at a small table that's barely big enough for his plates and all the papers stacked around it. A silver MacBook is perched precariously on one pile. His dark head is bent over a magazine, his chin rests on his upturned palm. His attention is rapt on whatever he's reading.

I clear my throat.

"Did you forget something?" he asks without looking up from whatever he's reading.

"It's me," I say haltingly.

He looks up and shoots to his feet so fast, his knees hit the table, rattling the crockery, scattering the papers and toppling his computer.

"Shit. Hi." He smiles and stoops to pick up the laptop. I rush forward and bend to help him.

"No, please, let me. Have a seat." He grabs my wrist to stop me from picking up an envelope. Our eyes meet and my senses come to attention. Have his eyes always been so dark and clear? Is his mouth even more plump than normal because he just woke up or did the light hide it from me the last time I saw him?

"Is there something on my face?" he asks.

I blink and look down at my hands. "No. Sorry. Hi."

"Is everything okay?" He tightens the belt on his dark blue robe. I've never noticed how prominent the veins in his arm are. Yum.

"Cassie?" His hand waves in front of my face.

I smile through my mortification. "Yes?"

His brows furrow. They're so *thick*. "Is everything okay?"

"Oh. Yeah. Everything is great. Thank you so much for asking."

"Do you...want to sit down?" He gestures at the chair behind me and I realize I'm still stooped over to pick up the papers that are no longer on the floor. My face burns with embarrassment. What is wrong with me?

"Yes, sorry." I give myself a mental slap and steer myself into the chair he pointed to. "I just wanted to say," I force my eyes to meet his and *dear heaven* why do they have to be so mesmerizing, "if you'd like to join me for breakfast or any meal at all, I'd like that." I actually meant to just say thank you, but I like the sound of it too much to pretend I don't mean it.

"I thought you wanted to be alone."

"Yeah, turns out eating alone isn't all that it's cracked up to be."

He smiles, a simple wide, happy smile and I return it. "I'd love to join you. As long as you're sure."

"I am."

I glance at his TV, which is paused, and gasp. "Oh my God. Are you watching *Alchemy of Souls*?"

A grin parts his lips. "For the second time."

"Really? How? I can't get it on any of the channels on my TV."

"Because only my TV has the VPN that allows me to watch it. Do you...want to join me?"

I glance around the room. There's nowhere to sit but his bed. But no worries that he'll make a move. "Are you sure you don't mind if I do?"

"Absolutely. We can even go back to whatever episode you're on."

"Okay. Next thing you're going to tell me is you have kettle corn and oat milk ice cream smoothies."

"I can get kettle corn. Oat milk might take a day or two."

I laugh, delighted and surprised. "Are you for real?"

He nods. "My money's even realer. Tell me what you want this week and I'll take care of it."

"Thank you. I don't know if you're really this nice or if you're buttering me up for some sort of ritual sacrifice, but either is cool."

He chuckles. "You're silly."

"Can I go grab my food and eat while we watch?"

"Yes. I've got some work to do, so I'll have to leave in an hour, but I'd love to watch an episode with you."

I couldn't have imagined a more perfect week if I tried. I've forgotten all about this mission of mine.

I walk back into my suite and find Ama, his assistant, standing outside the door. "Well, if it isn't my fairy godmother."

She doesn't crack a smile as she runs a slow critical eye over my pajama-clad body. "Leo is being nice because he's a decent human being, not because he's a fool. If you're looking for a way to turn this fiasco into an even bigger payday, don't. Better women than you have tried."

"I'm sure it didn't occur to you, but I have a life and plans of my own."

She rolls her eyes. "As if his money wouldn't make both of those things easier."

I mimic her eye roll "Money *is* nice. The more the better. But I wouldn't trade my life for more than I need and I certainly wouldn't pursue a man just because he has it."

She narrows her eyes at me. "Say whatever you want. Just know that if a single hair on that boy's head is hurt, I'll make sure you never have another job anywhere in the world. Do you understand?" The glint in her eye makes my soul tremble.

Okay…so she's intimidating. But I'm glad he has people around him who have his back especially when forces he can't see are working against him.

"I understand. I promise you have nothing to worry about." I say with a smile that's melted some icy hearts.

She doesn't even blink. "Good."

She's right. He's nice but he's no fool.

And neither am I.

* * * *

We only had breakfast together twice, but when Leo didn't join me this morning, I missed him.

I had to stop myself from going in search of him. Besides our meals together, and the episodes of *Alchemy of Souls* we've watched each evening, he's given me my space. I should respect his.

I'm taking the last sip of my creamy oat milk macchiato when Ama walks in and puts a note on the table.

Meet me on the second floor, in the closet of the 3rd bedroom on the right.

XO,

L

I frown at the XO.

What does *that* mean?

I scan the note again and my frown deepens. There isn't a third bedroom on the second floor. Unless the room with the locked door is a bedroom too. Even if I'd managed to find my way in here last week, Michel's intel would have led me astray.

I go back upstairs and walk to the third door on the right. The door is open and I step inside. I gasp and press a hand to my chest. "Wow." I breathe and turn a full circle to take it all in.

The room is like an atrium. It's got two glass walls that create a barrier between the living space and the trees and a small waterfall that surround it. A set of frameless French doors opens up onto a verandah. A set of stairs lead out to a small beach and a clear lagoon that appears to be sourced by the waterfall. I've never seen anything like it.

I have to drag myself away and back inside to the closet. I open the pocket doors on the left side of the room and my eyes nearly fall out of my head.

It looks like a department store. Everything is arranged by color. I walk along the rows of clothes that line the room's perimeter and run my fingers along them. Most of them still have price tags attached. I pull out everything that catches my eye and looks like it's dress appropriate.

I pick up the first dress. It's got a pale pink strapless mermaid style body and a black-beaded peek-a-boo of light blue and a black sequined bustier that looked like it would cut out right below my breasts.

Sexy.

I take it off the hanger and peek at the label on the inside. "Valentino. Wow."

It's in my size, but I don't know if designer sizes are the same as Target's.

I pull my t-shirt and bra over my head, slide my shorts over my hips, and step into the dress. It glides up my body easily.

I can't reach the zip, but I walk over to the mirror to look at myself in it. *Damn.* I look like I belong on a runway.

Who said clothes don't make the man?

I'm not down on myself or anything, but *nothing* has ever looked this good on me.

"It's perfect."

"Oh my God," I scream and jump nearly out of my skin. I whirl around and come face-to-face with Leo. "Why did you sneak up on me like that?"

He's leaning in the doorway, legs crossed at the ankles, watching me with that sexy as hell half smile. "Sorry. I thought you'd hear me come in. The dress fits." He nods at the dress.

I clutch at the gaping back self-consciously and twist my body to hide it from him. "It seems to. I'm not sure it will zip."

"Let me."

He places a hand on my shoulder and turns me around with a deft swing of his wrist. Before I can catch my breath from that, he nudges my hands away, pulls the zipper together, and starts dragging it up. The slide of his knuckles against my spine makes me shiver. It's been a long time since I've had my back to a man without feeling like I had to be on my guard. I hold my breath, not in fear, but in anticipation.

The tips of his fingers brush my back as he drags the zipper up and it feels like a prelude to something. But when he gets to the top, he squeezes either side of my neck briefly, and lets go. He stands back and I turn to the mirror.

The dress fits like a glove. It's a little snug in the bust and thighs, but not enough to be uncomfortable.

"It looks good," he says.

I smooth a hand down my hips. "Yeah, I'll wear this."

"Yes, you will. The color is great on your skin."

I stroke the skirt and sigh. I've never felt anything so soft and light. "Are you sure? This looks really special."

"It is. The creative director at Armani designed it for Valentino himself. My mother couldn't pull it off and never wore it. Only Zendaya has worn one and hers wasn't this color."

"It's so beautiful. I couldn't."

"I want you to wear it."

I eye the dress. "I'd be afraid to damage it."

"Why? It's just a dress. It was made to be worn. If it gets damaged, we'll repair it or just get another one."

My eyes go wide. "It's priceless."

He nods. "Whether it cost five dollars or fifty thousand, it's a garment. It was designed for human bodies to wear and sometimes, even ruin. What's priceless is the experience you have while you're *wearing* it. If you don't like it, fine. But if it's simply because you place more value on the dress than the person who might wear it, let this be the first step to breaking free of that kind of thinking."

I want to push back on his characterization of my hesitation toward wearing the dress. But he's not wrong. I *do* think it's too good for me to wear, but he's also right that *not* wearing it is a waste. "Okay, all of that is easy for you say."

"It's just a thing. One of a kind but not irreplaceable."

"Yes, it is."

"No. It's not. Let me show you something." He walks over to the wall and pushes the clothes blocking it aside to reveal a small door. My heart skips a beat.

The safe.

His back blocks my view as he pulls it open and reaches inside, but I'm certain he didn't enter a code.

"This set is from Bulgaria." He pulls out a diamond choker adorned with large pink, purple and teal stones and a sparkly cuff bracelet. "It's insured for twenty million dollars and one of a kind. But it doesn't mean anything. At least not to me."

He puts the jewelry down and reaches back inside the safe. "Now *this*," he says with a flours and extends his arm to me, palm open.

My heart skips a beat and then starts beating so fast my head spins. I blink to be sure I'm not seeing things. It's the ring I was sent here to steal.

"This was my father's." He plucks it out of his palm and holds it up to the light.

It's even less impressive in person. "It's the ring that the men in his family passed down to their oldest son. It's worth nothing, I might be able to sell it for a few hundred dollars."

"If you're lucky," I quip and we both laugh. But my mind is whirling.

I don't understand why someone would pay me so much money to steal this family heirloom. If his father *passed* it to him...I whip around to face him. "Wait, does that mean your father died?"

The humor in his expression disappears. He drops the ring back into his palm and stares at it. "Yes, a year ago." He swallows hard and fingers the ring with a reverent touch that makes my heart ache. It's priceless to him.

I keep my eyes on the jewelry, tracing the outline of it with my finger so he won't suspect that I'm avoiding his gaze. My mind is whirling with questions and doubt. "Why don't you wear it?" The question comes out before I realize I'm going to ask it.

He blinks like I splashed water in his face. "I don't…I don't know." He puts the ring down next to the jewelry and steps a huge step backward. "I have to go. I'll ask Hannah to come up and help you out of the dress. Sorry." He tries to smile but the turmoil in his eyes gives him away.

"I'm sorry about your dad." I close the distance between us in a few steps and wrap my arms around him in a hug. He needs one more than anyone I've seen in a long time.

"Uh—thank you." He stiffens and pats me awkwardly but doesn't pull away until I let go.

He clears his throat. "Okay, I'll send Hannah in now." He turns to leave again.

"I'll see you later?" I call after him.

He pauses mid-step and turns back to face me. He meets my eye but the emotions I'd seen play across his face are gone. "Sorry, I can't join you tonight. I've got a meeting." He has the grace to look away when he tells that lie.

"Oh, okay." I tamp down my disappointment. Our meals together have been the highlight of my week.

"Enjoy your last day of doing whatever you want," he says. "The stylist will be here in the morning. The team from the resort will be here at noon to help you get ready. If you need anything else, let Hannah know."

"I think you've thought of everything."

"I have. Always do. You'll see." And with that cryptic message and curt nod, he turns and leaves.

I turn to look at the jewelry he left sitting out. Instead of jubilation at this stroke of good luck, I'm panicking. I hold it in until Hannah comes in to help me out of the dress. She puts the jewelry back in the safe without a lock and leaves me alone with my dilemma and newly acquired conscience.

I should never have agreed to his proposal. And I shouldn't have spent all that time with him. I go back to the closet and open the safe. I stare at the ring but can't bring myself to take it.

This feels too easy. And now that I know what it means to him, wrong.

I cover my face with my hands. *Shit.* He's the one who is being robbed. But why does it feel like I'm a mouse in a maze, being guided by cheese instead of my good sense?

I should have aborted this mission.

Living here won't make it easier to do what I came to do. If I could take the ring now and leave I would. But even *If* I could get off this island without Michel's help, I don't know how far I'd get. Leo knows my first name and what I look like. When he discovers the ring is missing, he'll connect the dots and know it was me that took it. A man who can afford a house like this can afford to hire someone to track me down fast.

What the hell have I gotten myself into?

7

Charm

LEO

Charisma comes easy.

I get it from my father.

I watched him use it like a weapon to usurp a government, bend its people to his will, and make them fall in love with him.

He lived for nights like this.

Glamour, conversation, music, intimacy, meaningful connections.

He entertained every evening unless he was traveling. Watching him work the room was a master class in making people do whatever you want by making them feel like they were the only person in the whole world while he talked to them. His energy was endless. He danced until his partners begged for a break. He'd let them go and pull up another person. It didn't matter if he'd been in tense conversations all day.

The minute he stepped into his house, he went from head of state to life of the party. People stopped bowing and scraping and instead danced to his tune.

I fell in love with the French horn and Ray Barretto, Salsa and life in this house.

The first week I spent here felt like walking through my own ghost story.

And yet there is something about this evening…these people and the woman on my arm that remind me of the good old days when the house had been full of music and light and laughter and the only glass that shattered was from crystal champagne flutes that slipped out of drink-loosened grips.

There's a knock on the partially open door to the hallway. "Can I come in?"

I turn to face Cassie, my mind still occupied with thoughts of my father. "Of course. It's almost—" My eyes land on her and my mind goes blank.

She's a vision. I've never seen anyone more beautiful.

Her hair is braided in the Fulani style my nieces are a fan of. But on her, they're sexy as hell. The way they leave the exquisite bone structure and flawless deep brown skin that compose her unforgettable face screams confidence. The braids cascade around her shoulders like palm fronds on a stiff breeze. The tiny gold and clear glass beads strung onto the end of them glint like silver and gold in the light.

The dress is exquisite on her. She looks like Persephone rising and bringing a fertile spring in her wake. Her lips are slicked with a gloss that's a shade lighter than her golden-brown skin and outrageously sexy.

Her shoulders and arms glow as if she's walking with a spotlight on her as she approaches me. My mouth waters.

"You look…incredible." I lift her hand to my mouth and press a kiss to the back of it.

"Thank you." She smiles with a coyness that's unexpected and charming beyond measure. "You look really nice, too."

I have to glance in the mirror to remember what I'm wearing. The royal-blue Tom Ford suit was a gift from my mother. It's the same blue as in the Seychelles flag. The lightweight silk is lined with a canary yellow satin fabric that's only visible when I take the jacket on and off. "Thank you."

"So, anything I need to know about tonight?"

"Just be yourself. If by some miracle one of the people you meet stops talking long enough to ask you about yourself, answer honestly."

She fiddles with the delicate gold band on her finger and looks away. "Okay. Maybe I should tell you a little about myself so we don't end up saying things that contradict themselves?"

"Hmmm, good thinking. Have you done this before?" I ask.

She gives me a half smile. "I just like to be prepared."

"Okay. Go ahead. Tell me all about Cassie Why."

That earns me a smile and her shoulders lose some of their stiffness. "I'm a student."

"What are you studying?"

"I'm in my last year of college. I'm pre-law. I'm 21, an Aquarius, born and raised in Texas."

"What part of Texas?"

"Why?" She quirks an eyebrow and her lips turn down.

"One of the people who will be here tonight—he's actually one of my father's protégés—has an office there."

"Texas is a pretty big place. But still, tell me his name. I'd hate for him to be the one-in-a-million guy who knows my boyfriend or something."

"Your what?" I ask, my vision darkening with irritation that she's not single. "You didn't mention you had a boyfriend."

She scowls. "Why would I mention it? I'm working. We're not *really* dating. And it's not any of your business."

Her words are the cold splash of reality I need.

She's exactly right.

"His name's Chudi Okoye."

Her frown deepens. "What does he look like?"

"Why? Do you know someone named Chudi?"

She scoffs. "Ummm. I know *two* Chudi's." She holds up two fingers in my face.

"Are you Nigerian?"

"I grew up in Houston. My mother is Ghanaian and is the world's biggest busybody. She knows a lot of people, and I can't tell you how many West Africans I've met in the most random places that remember me from the one time they came to lunch at my parents' house while I was growing up."

I chuckle at how parallel that sounds to my existence.

"Anyway, Both Chudi's I know are tall. One of them is a dancer, the other a banker."

I snort. "I think we're safe. This Chudi is 5'5" and an energy minister in Nigeria now."

"Definitely don't know him. Zero chances of him telling my mother I was posted up with a billionaire in the Seychelles when she thinks I'm glamping in Tulum."

The meaning of her words wraps around my throat in a very irritating reminder that I don't know this woman and she should be handled with caution. If she can lie to her mother, she can lie to anyone.

"Why would you need to lie to your mother about what you're doing?"

She shrugs and for the first time since we've been acquainted, she doesn't meet my eyes. "It's hard to explain. She is set in her ways."

I am not one to throw stones from my glass house so I don't push for more details.

I take her hand. "Let's go down. Our guests have been here for half an hour. Perfect time for us to make our entrance."

"Entrance?" She raises an eyebrow. "Like...in *Coming to America?*" She laughs.

I should be offended.

My father might have been. Biz certainly would have been.

But I find it...refreshing to be with someone who sees how absurd some of these things are.

I wish...I'd met her somewhere else.

When I wasn't still caught in this cosplay directed by my stepmother.

My conviction that this will be the first and last time grows as I see all of this through her eyes.

"I'm glad there'll be at least one person present who lives outside the bubble of state affairs and social politics."

She laughs. "No worries about me having any insight into any of *that or* people like you." She snorts a laugh.

"Like who?" I don't know why it bothers me so much to be lumped in with them.

"With a house like this, ambassadors, and ministers and Valentino. They all say a lot about who you are before you even open your mouth."

My chuckle is dry. I wish I could argue with her without sounding like a poor little rich boy. "You'll find out tonight that my uncle was a head of state when he died. But I am and have always been, a private citizen."

She blinks and draws away from me. "Head of state?"

"Yes."

She gasps. "Wow. Like President, Prime Minister?"

I nod. "We can talk about it more later." Hopefully never.

The lines between her eyebrows furrow. "You can't just stop there. Tell me more."

"Our guests are waiting. I'm sorry." I hold my breath and wait for her to push back.

"Nothing to be sorry about. It's none of my business anyway."

"It's not. But for some reason, I feel like telling you."

"We can pick it up whenever you're ready." She smiles, stands back and holds her arms out. "You sure I look good?"

Like a hungry man's feast. "More than."

She smooths her hands over the body-hugging bodice and furrows her brows apprehensively. "And, you're a big deal. Are you sure I don't look... less than someone who you would normally be with?"

I put my hands on her shoulders and turn her to face the full-length mirror next to the door. "Everyone here is the child or grandchild, niece or nephew of a president, prime minister, ambassador, cabinet member, Supreme Court justice, etc. There will be name dropping and pretty ostentatious displays of wealth. I apologize in advance. It's embarrassing because we get painted with the same brush, and not all of us are entitled, self-absorbed assholes. You are interesting, self-made and smart. So lift your chin and walk in there like you know you deserve to be there, too."

Our eyes meet in the mirror and hers glisten with tears. "Are you real? Because that's the nicest thing anyone has ever said to me. And you don't know me well enough to know these things, but they're the things I believe about myself deep down, too. I think. Or at least what I want to be true."

"I mean, I don't know you. But that's the energy you give. It's in you. So if your life doesn't reflect that, make it so. You have the power to create the life you love. You've only got this one, and every day is a gift. It can change like that." I snap my fingers.

"That's morbid."

"That's life."

I take a step toward her. "And for the record, I remembered your name because I haven't been able to forget it. I've had a hard time keeping my eyes off you."

She blinks like I've splashed water on her face. "What? Off me?"

"Yes. You're kind of a mess. But I can see the method in it. And the fact that your integrity has no price." *And you're beautiful.* "And I think…you might feel the same because I've seen the way you look at me, too."

She flushes.

I force myself to stay where I am. "I'm trying to be respectful. And not make you feel uncomfortable. I know you're not single."

"I might as well be." She takes a step toward me. "You're not wrong about the way I look at you. At first…it was because you look like…Tyson Beckford. But now… it's because you're kind." She smooths my tie and pats my chest. "There's not a lot of that in this world. It's very attractive. And so are you. I know this is just make-believe. But I'm going to enjoy pretending a man like you is my boyfriend."

"A man like me?"

"You're cool as fuck."

"I am," I quip.

"I'm serious."

"I hope you're right. I'm going to need my cool tonight."

"Let's go wow them, Wild Card."

"After you, Ms. Why." I wave for her to walk ahead of me.

She takes my hand and laces our fingers together. When our palms meet, it feels familiar. Like we've done this before.

She gives me the sexiest little grin and squeezes my hand. "No. Let's go in together."

* * * *

If Dante's circles of Hell were real, this party would surely be one of them.

The entire Afropolitan elite had been invited and they weren't the crowd you cancelled last minute on. I wish my mother was here, but my father was the only reason she stayed in the Seychelles for so long. Once he died, she left and swore to never come back.

I know these people well. We're a group of first-generation children with American, British, Aussie, or European passports, West African heritage, and no true home.

Some of us were at the same boarding schools.

Some of us met at university in America, England, or Canada.

We have different accents, languages, and postures for every world we occupy. Tonight, when it's just us, we can be our mashed-up selves. At this table, no one is going to ask "where are you from?" or have our accents mimicked or corrected.

Our hierarchy is based on pure economic and political power. An abundance of just one of those is enough to elevate you into the sphere of the elite, both of them are enough to put you at the pinnacle of society.

People still think my father was my uncle. That my elevated status is due to being his nephew—the son of his favorite sister, who was widowed while pregnant with me.

My mother was really the love of his life.

There are few truly well-kept secrets in politics.

But my paternity is one of them.

No one is willing to risk the wrath of my stepmother. She, like my mother, is the daughter of a very rich businessman.

Unlike my mother, she was married to the father of her children, politically savvy, and more popular with the people than her husband.

I don't know why she *really* asked me to host this event, and I'm not sure why I said yes, but once I did, I was determined for it to go off perfectly.

The rectangle dinner table runs the length of the room. A centerpiece of frangipani and votive candles down the center separates diners sitting across from each other. The lighting is low, the music is dimmed to background. The pool has been converted to a dance floor and the band is setting up for the night's festivities. I can't wait for the night to be over.

"So, Leo," one of my friends interrupts us and I give Cassie an apologetic smile and turn toward the familiar deep voice.

"Delé, nice to see you."

He quirks an eyebrow and grins. "Are you sure? You've barely spoken to anyone at the table all night."

"Can you blame me?" I tip my head in Cassie's direction.

She smiles demurely, but takes a sip of champagne served with dinner in lieu of speaking. I'm mesmerized by the way her lips cling to the glass and the smudge of lipstick they leave behind. "Surely you understand."

Delé slaps me on the back. "Not a bit. And very nice given Mona's presence."

I glance to the other end of the table where my ex-girlfriend and her new husband are sitting. She may like drama, but she's a product of this world and knows better than to cause a scene in the presence of so many important people.

"You've done your uncle proud."

I give him a stiff smile. We were in the same house at boarding school and I never liked him. "I hope so. I can't take credit. Ama really made it happen. I just showed up."

"Don't be modest, darling." Cassie strokes my hand and beams at me like I'm the sun itself. "He had a hand in every aspect of this evening."

I was already pleased with her performance, but that just earned her a nice bonus.

And even though she only said it in the spirit of being a supportive girlfriend, the praise feels good.

Delé gives her a tight smile. "How nice." He gives her a once-over and turns back to me.

"I'm sorry about the old man by the way." He signals for the waiter and gives me a sympathetic smile, leaning back so the waiter can fill his champagne glass. "But you must be relieved."

"Excuse me?" Cassie says, raising her voice loud enough to draw attention from the diners further down the table.

I flinch. "What do you mean?"

"That you can come home. Join the family business."

I laugh, but there's nothing behind it. "I have zero interest in that."

"You've been in America too long. You've forgotten the order of things. Come home, find a wife, start a family. Stat."

"The order of things is exactly what I'm trying to forget."

He leans forward. His expression growing serious. "But…now that he's dead, you can come out of the shadows, right? No one cares who your father *really* is now. You deserve a place in the official family."

The silence comes in a wave that rushes down the table and creates an awkward, pregnant pause before conversations resume.

I keep my eyes on my plate and count to ten.

The rumors about my paternity are out there.

I knew it, but no one has dared bring it up in front of me.

"Was that meant to embarrass me?" I ask.

His smile fades. "No. Of course not."

He's lying, but he wouldn't dare own it.

Fifteen years ago, it would have worked. But today, I barely feel the hit.

I look Delé in the eye, and smile. "I know you don't have as many options and resources as I do. So, this might be hard for you to understand." I take a sip of my water and give him a steely smile. "I'm twenty-five years old, and a billionaire. Why would I limit myself to one place or person when the entire world is my playground?"

I hate when people force me to be a dick. I'm as cool as they come. I don't look for beef. But if it looks for me I don't run from it. One thing I learned from my father was to make sure people understood what they could and couldn't get away with.

From the word go.

And I see the change in Delé's posture as my words sink in.

I was the butt of their jokes. But now, I'm a billion-dollar wild card. One word from me could change his life for better or worse. And now that I've reminded him of that, he'll treat me the way he used to treat my brothers.

His eyes narrow and his smile is caustic. "It's nice to see you looking so well, Leo. Can't wait to see what you do next."

I turn away to face Cassie and smile even though the blood is rushing in my ears. "Sorry you had to hear that."

She smiles back and instead of the pity I expected to see, there's respect in her eyes "I'm not. I like the way you talk, Leo." Her smile is suggestive.

I glance at my watch and then around the table. Everyone, without exception, is engaged in conversation. Dinner plates have been cleared and I've reached my limit.

I don't know how I put up with these people for so long, but this is the last time I'm going to sit here and pretend. My father is gone. I don't owe the family that shunned me anything. Not when, even now, they won't acknowledge me.

I hold a hand out to Cassie. "Let's go."

"With pleasure," she murmurs and slips her hand into mine. I tap my knife against the crystal flute of my glass to get the attention of my guests.

They quiet down instantly, all of their eyes trained on me as if they really care what I'm about to say. They don't, but they've been raised to respect the hierarchy. And despite my illegitimacy, I'm at the top of this one. "Thank you all for coming and excuse me for leaving while the night is still young, but it's been a very stressful month and it's all catching up to me.

"Please stay—enjoy until it's time for departure. The people carriers that brought you here will be back at 11 p.m. The ferry back to the Mahé will leave every hour on the hour, starting at 8 a.m. and going until 1 p.m. If you miss the ferry, you will need to extend your stay at the lodge."

Murmurs of "of course" and "absolutely" ripple through the room.

"All the best, Leo. I hope you get everything you deserve." Mona raises her glass and tips it with a sardonic smile. "And you," she says and nods at Cassie with a smile like the cat who got the cream. "He's a commitment-phobe."

Cassie's hand tightens around mine. She giggles and nestles against me. "I'm just using him for orgasms and bragging rights. So I'm good."

A ripple of shocked laughter runs down the table and I look at her in horror.

She winks and grins. "Right?"

She clamps her cool hand around the back of my neck, and lifts up onto her toes, raising her soft lips toward mine. I'm suddenly aware of how much I want to kiss her. I drop my head and meet her halfway, my lips tingling even before we touch.

And yet, I'm not prepared for the intensity of need it ignites.

She may have been doing this to defend my pride, but when my arms circle her waist to pull her closer, her fingers clutch my head, and she's kissing me for real.

We go from sweet to sizzle in 2.4 seconds and everything but her and the physical connection we're sharing disappears.

She tastes so good, I can't kiss her deep enough. She grips my lapel and presses her soft body against mine. I groan and cup her ass.

A loud cough penetrates the void I fell into and my eyes pop open and dart to the left.

Reality skids in like a needle on a scratched record. I remember where I am.

I pull my mouth off hers and step back but keep my hand on her lower back as she sways. The entire table is watching us slack-jawed. I curse my loss of control. My father may be dead, but his wife and my siblings aren't.

One look at Mona and I know there's no way this won't get around.

Those NDAs are iron clad and my brother has been the enforcer for those who break them for a decade. There will be no leaks to the press, but this will be fodder for the small but voracious gossip mill.

So I give it a good greasing. "Grief is weird. And she's beautiful. What can I say? It's a full moon."

They chuckle and nod as if they agree.

"Goodnight. Enjoy the rest of the evening and thank you again for being my guests."

Cassie blows a kiss and waves like she's the queen.

God, I *really* like this woman.

I hold my hand out, she slips hers into it, and we walk out together.

8

Praslin

Cassie

My heart is racing as we walk out of there. I've never had to hold myself back as hard as I did tonight. My claws were aching for a taste of that Delé character. I don't know the story on Leo's dad. I'm not going to ask because it's not my business. And because I know having shitty, messy, irresponsible parents doesn't make you the same. But I hate that he has to deal with people like that taking shots at him.

"So, since you *clearly* hated that, and have spent the week letting me do things I love, I'd like to spend our last night together doing something *you* really love."

His expression goes from stoic to soft. "Really?"

"Yup."

"And..." He's been taking care of me all week. I'm about to take care of him. "A little birdie told me you like Angelique Kidjo."

"Who told you that?"

I waggle my eyebrows when he frowns.

"Hannah and I had a whole week. It doesn't matter who told me. All that matters is that Angelique Kijoo is playing live in Praslin. Tonight."

"Tonight?"

"The show doesn't start for another hour...what do you say we go?"

"Do you have tickets?"

"I got us covered."

His frown deepens. "That's not concrete enough for me."

The edge of panic in his voice at the idea of a detail being out of place.

"I promise, we'll have a way in. All you have to do is get us there."

"Praslin is about fifteen minutes away by boat."

"And do you have a boat?" I ask.

"Yes. Of course. We're on an island."

"Okay, smart ass." I bump his hip with mine. "Do you know how to drive it?"

He scoffs and crosses his arms over his chest. "Yes. But I don't want to go all the way there if we can't get in."

I hold my hand, pinky finger out, toward him. "Trust me."

"Do I have a choice?" he mutters but hooks his finger through mine.

I chuckle. "Not if you want to have fun tonight."

"I'm not sure our definitions of fun are the same."

"Let's go find out."

9

Fun

Leo

I have never gone anywhere without some sort of security in tow. My detail is light and once they sweep my house, they retire to the resort to sleep. As soon as they were gone, we drove a golf cart to the marina and got into the boat my father named after my mother, Anowa, and sailed for Praslin. It's only a fifteen-minute journey but I didn't like making it in the dark. I made a note to find us a place to spend the night as soon we docked in the marina.

We hiked, her in her designer gown and heels, me in my suit, up the hill to the club where the concert had already started. We turned a few heads but no one did more than compliment us on our getups.

I followed the lead of the enchantress who could lead me straight to Hell without much more than a come-hither look. My attraction to her has grown wings since this weekend. I lied when I said she wasn't my type. It felt like the best way to create distance. But now, I could kick myself because I'm wildly attracted and feeling like when we get back stateside, I want to see her again.

I like her company. It's easy and she's as calm as she is chaotic.

We arrive at the club, one of the biggest on this island, and the music spills out into the street. "Okay, we're going to flirt with the lady at the door. Whoever she swings for, closes the deal."

I grab her hand. "What the hell are you talking about?"

"Umm, you're a hot guy. Don't tell me you've never smiled your way into a club, or party, or concert?"

"Why would I need to? I'm a VIP. I get tickets to whatever I want."

She rolls her eyes. "Well your VIP status won't work here. It's not the Ritz. Follow my lead."

She reaches inside her dress, cups her breasts and lifts them. Then she slides her arm through mine and strolls over to the blonde, bombshell Brigitte Nielsen look-alike guarding the door.

"Hi, did the show already start?" Cassie smiles, wide and big and I swear light shoots out from her eyes.

The blonde who I would have sworn had never smiled a day in her life, looks Cassie up and down, and her stern expression softens. "Well aren't you a cutie. American?"

"A nice one, I swear," Cassie says with a breathy voice. I look at her sharply.

"And aren't you two a lovely couple." The woman eyes me a little too hard for my liking.

"Oh. We're not a couple," Cassie purrs.

The woman's smile widens and she turns to me. "I like him."

I take a step back. "I'm hers." I say and put an arm around her waist.

Cassie smiles at me but there's murder in her eyes. "What are you doing?" she hisses.

"What I should have done right away." I look back at the woman. "I have cash. How much do you want to let us in?"

She flashes an impressively predatory grin. "I like cash even more. Five hundred each. Dollars. US," she adds for clarity.

"No way," Cassie gasps.

"Here." I reach into my pocket, pull out my money clip and peel off ten brand new hundreds.

"I don't want to see Angelique Kijoo this badly," Cassie says.

"I do." I hand over the money and tug her in after me. "Now, come and give me the night you promised."

*　*　*　*

It's after midnight when we stumble out of the smoke-filled club. The starch in my collar is somewhere in a pool of sweat on the floor. And so is every inhibition I walked in there with. Cassie showed me the time of my life. I've never been to a live show. Cassie is on my back, her heels dangling from my fingers. "Ms. Why, you're heavier than you look."

"Stop calling me that. Where are we going?"

"We can't go back to Le Digue tonight. Let's go get a couple of rooms for the night."

"Oh, I'm so glad you said that. I'm too tired for a boat ride."

I snort a laugh. "I didn't realize riding a boat was so strenuous."

"Well now you do. Do you know where you're going?"

"No, but he will."

I raise my arm to hail a cab and put her down before bundling us inside. "Can you take us to the closest hotel?"

When we stumble up to the counter of the decent enough Wyndham, Cassie has strapped her shoes back on and leans on me to take some of the weight off her aching feet.

"Hello, welcome to the Wyndham. Are you checking in?"

"Yes, we need two rooms."

The woman grimaces. "We've only got one room and it's got a queen bed. Is that okay?"

"It's fine," we say at the same time and glance at each other with equally surprised smiles.

We make our way up to the room in total silence but I could cut the tension between us with a knife. That kiss back there was... something. But she's leaving and I've got no business doing what I'm thinking about doing.

10

Caution

LEO

As soon as I close the door behind us, the lights come on. The room is fine—clean with a bed, dresser and television.

"This is cozy." Cassie drops her small bag on the bed and turns a full circle.

I strip off my jacket and hang it on the back of the door.

She kicks her heels off and walks over to look out of the window. "There are literally no bad views here."

"Not a one." I join her and stare out into the moonlit night. The hotel is elevated and the sky and ocean collide and appear to become one. "I can't believe we actually did that."

She laughs. "Stick with me kid, you'll start believing."

"So…did you have fun tonight?" she asks, still facing the ocean.

"Once we were away from the party, it was nothing but. Thank you."

"I had fun, too. You're welcome."

We fall into a comfortable silence and I enjoy the moment of nothing but contentment. And then as I always do when my mind is quiet, I replay the evening and remember that there are things I want to say to this woman.

"Mona is my ex."

She sighs, resting her head on my arm. "When did it end?"

"We broke up a year ago. I'm not important enough to be her husband. She wants to be a first lady."

"Wow. Really? I didn't even know that was a thing you could aspire to."

"It's not a common ambition. But it was hers."

"So, that's why you broke up? Because you're not the president of a country? Her husband is?"

"Minister of Foreign Affairs, and he's a favorite in the next election."

"So why is she here?"

I shrug. "They were invited but didn't RSVP so I don't know."

"Well, she was eye fucking you and he was trying to kill you with eye daggers so I'd say you got away unscathed."

"I don't know why she was so rude to you."

"Nothing makes you feel worse than seeing you ex thriving with another person on their arm."

"Especially another person who looks like *you*."

She rolls her eyes. "You didn't even notice me until I put on this dress."

"I noticed you the minute we bumped into each other. And I haven't been able to see anything else since. Except for all the things I want to do to you."

She sucks in a breath. I turn to her with a neutral expression on my face. I don't know why my lips are so loose with this woman. But I don't regret saying it.

Her eyes are wide—but not with repulsion or fear.

I think...that's excitement lighting them and turning her lips up at the corners.

"Really?" Her surprise is charming.

"Why? Have *you* been thinking of ways to kill me?"

"No. I've been thinking of ways to undress you. I've been thinking of ways to get you to let me." She takes a step toward me after every sentence.

"Keep giving the middle finger to assholes and being such a good girl for me, and I'm yours."

"A good girl?" She recoils and curls her lip. "Does that actually *work* for you?"

"Never fails."

"I'll be the first, then."

"Will you?" I lift my eyebrow and skim my bottom lip with my teeth as I take her in.

"You're not my type." She tosses a braid over her shoulder.

"Liar."

"And I'm not yours either," she says but she doesn't move away when I close the space between us.

"I'm a liar, too."

"I don't want to sleep with you," she whispers.

"Then tell me to stop."

Her back presses against the wall behind us and I put a hand on either side of her head.

I look down into her dark amber eyes and she looks up into mine.

Her breaths come hard and fast, and her chest rises and falls against mine. "This is crazy."

I lower my head and lick her full lower lip. "Yes, crazy. Just like you."

She sighs and her lashes flutter. "*Just*. Like. Me."

God, she's so fucking *real*. And I'm done talking. Our mouths meet and she opens for me like she's been waiting.

Our lips duel and dart.

Like the kiss at the table, this one sparks so hot. But without the weight of the audience, we're even more feral.

I drop to my knees and push aside the voluminous fabric of her dress until I get to her skin. She's wearing chocolate lace panties. I don't have to press my nose to them to smell her arousal. But I do anyway. The damp fabric makes me want to pound my chest. She's so wet. For me. I cover her with my mouth and suck the plump lips of her pussy through the fabric of her panties.

She gasps. Her hands grip my shoulders. "Oh my God, Leo."

I slide her panties down and she steps out of them. I stuff them into my pocket and lift her leg and drop it onto my shoulder.

I could spend an hour just looking at her cunt. But my mouth is watering and I want to know what she tastes like when she comes.

I hold her open. Her clit looks like a fucking flower. I lick the sensitive nub and listen for how she responds. She lets out a sharp cry as I flick it over and over with the tip of my tongue.

"Leo, suck it. Please, God, I need to come."

I chuckle. I'm just getting started, but if she needs it now, I won't drag it out. I close my lips over her and suck, soft and slow at first.

"That's it, that's it. Yes, don't move, ugh. Don't stop. God help me." She writhes against the wall and I hold her bucking hips in place while she unravels around me until she stops.

She cups my head. "Leo. Jesus. It's been so long. I'd forgotten."

Her words hit me like a splash of ice-cold water.

She has a man.

Fuck.

"Oh my God. I'm so sorry. I got carried away."

"So…you aren't going to make good on all that foreplay?" She raises her eyebrows and runs her tongue over her lips.

I get to my feet and let her dress fall back down. "No condoms."

She deflates and lets her head fall back on a sigh. "Ah. And that is one mountain that can't be moved. No baby making allowed," she mutters.

"You don't want kids?"

"Not with a man I've only known for a week."

I cock my head at the bed. "I'm knackered, let's lay down."

She nods and strolls over, her hands working on the zipper.

"Let me." I brush her hands away.

She raises her arms over her head so that I reach the zip that starts right under her arm.

"So you want kids eventually?" I ask, trying to distract myself as her smooth, flawless skin is revealed by the parting zipper.

"I don't know. I honestly haven't thought that far ahead."

"All done." I step away and turn my back as she shimmies out of the dress. She's not wearing anything underneath. She sits, leans back on her elbows, as comfortable in her skin as she was in her clothes. Her body is incredible.

"Do you want kids?" she asks. I loosen my tie and tug it off.

"Not until I have something worth passing down."

"Uh...you have like a whole island and a billion dollars."

I cringe when I remember what I said to Delé. "I mean something more than material things. And I don't know the first thing about kids. I was hardly one myself." I throw my shirt over the chair and take off my trousers.

"I understand that.." She tucks a lock of hair behind her ear and flashes a sweet, sultry smile. "Anyway, it's probably best. My relationship is on the rocks, but it's not over. I need to figure out one thing before I start another, you know?"

"Yeah. I understand. And agree." As much as I hate thinking about her going home to this guy, I'm glad she respects him even if she's not in love with him anymore. "But I'd like to see you again. If you'd like to see me."

The smile I'd hoped to see doesn't come.

Her eyes dart away.

My stomach sinks. "Or not?"

Her eyes come back to mine, worry furrowing her brow. "No, I want to see you. It's just...I'm like...your average first-generation American. No lifestyles of the rich and famous for me."

"Okay, I live well below my means. I'm surrounded by luxury like this all the time. I like that you're regular."

"Great. Glad being regular has finally paid off." She scowls.

I press a kiss to her temple. "Me too. So, is that a yes?"

She smiles so wide her eyes narrow to slits. "Yes, Leo. I'd love to see you when you're back stateside."

I pull back the covers of the bed and she climbs in. I try to avert my gaze from her body. Sleeping next to her like this and not touching her is going to be sweet torture.

She scoots to the middle of the bed and I climb in after. She drapes a leg over my thighs and rests her head on my shoulder. I am so used to sleeping alone, I'd forgotten how nice it feels to curl up with another warm body.

I close my eyes against the dark and savor the feeling.

I can't believe she's leaving tomorrow.

"Where will you be in a month?"

"Starting law school at in Austin."

"You said. That's amazing. I thought about law school."

"Decided against it?"

"I'm thinking about it. I studied economics and politics. But I'm leaning toward an MBA."

"Do you know where you want to do it?"

"Harvard."

Her eyebrows shoot up. "Wow."

I wave off the awe in her expression. "I'm a legacy admission."

"Your dad went to Harvard, too?"

I nod. "Yeah, and my mom. That's where they met. And as my mother would jokingly say, ruined each other's lives."

She chuckles. "That's so cool. My parents met in college, too. How long were they together?"

"Almost thirty years."

"Do you have any brothers or sisters?" The question is a swift kick in my gut.

"Yeah, I have two brothers and two sisters, but I'm only close with one of them." It hurts to say that aloud. But it also feels good to be honest about it. I haven't talked to anyone about my father honestly. Not even my mother because I can't deal with her guilt over it all on top of my grief. I find it very easy to talk to Cassie.

She puts a hand on my shoulder. "Oh, Leo. I'm so sorry. I shouldn't have asked so flippantly."

I focus on her face again. Her smile is so comforting. "It's okay."

She shakes her head, her eyes glimmer in the dimly lit darkness of the room. "I'm always curious how other families whose parents met young have turned out, my parents are married and probably shouldn't be."

"That sucks, too. My family...is complicated. Messy even."

"Mine is just straightforward and dysfunctional. No mess, no nuance. Reversed roles, terrible communication, and shitty boundaries."

"Reversed roles?" I ask.

"I've been taking care of my parents since I was twelve and took online home economics class to figure out how to."

"Don't they work?"

"They do. But they're terrible with money and never had enough at the end of the month. I hated living that way so I took over paying bills, gave everyone an allowance, and started a savings account for them."

"At twelve?" I ask shocked.

"Necessity is the mother of every early independent child."

The words hit the wall of resolve around the secrets I keep. I blow out of a harsh breath and run my hand along the curve of her head. "That is *very* true."

"I know. And for me, survival wasn't good enough. I think I was born with an instinct to thrive. I wanted more." She yawns and snuggles closer, her hair tickling my chin.

We lay silent in the dark.

As I hold her, my heart feels too big for my chest. I want more, too.

More than a lie of life. For someone to know the truth.

She could be that someone.

But first, she has to know what she's getting into.

And the clock is ticking. My pulse speeds up as I practice the words in my head. I've never said them aloud. Never wanted to.

But lying here in the dark, holding a stranger who feels like someone I've known forever, the need for *her* to know who I really am is overwhelming.

"I told you that the resort and house were my uncle's. And that he was a head of state."

"Mmhmm." She nods.

"That's not true."

She's silent. I brace for her to stiffen, move away from me.

But she doesn't.

"Okay. I'm listening," she says softly.

I inhale, fill my lungs with her sweet smell and let it out. "The man I called uncle was really my father. And my mother wasn't his wife."

Her eyes grow wide, her mouth drops open. "Wow. So he *had* a wife...and your mom was like his mistress?"

That word makes me cringe still. "Yes. Openly. Before he was married. I was born a few months after my half-brother, Bismark."

"Wow, how was that?"

I put my free hand between the back of my head and my pillow.

"My parents were together for almost thirty years. He loved my mother. But his wife was his closest political advisor and incredibly powerful in her own right. Divorcing her was out of the question."

"And you grew up with him?"

"Yes and no. He sent my mother to America to have me. His wife insisted. But when he became president, and no one was above him, he brought us back. I was six. And I had to call him uncle in public."

"Oh my God, Leo." The horror in her voice is touching.

"It's okay. It wasn't easy. For me or my mother, but I had a good life. And if his will is a reflection of how he feels about me, I was actually his favorite," I say with humor I don't feel.

He left me fifty percent of his six-billion-dollar personal fortune. The other fifty percent was shared in equal proportion between my three other siblings. Their shares were fortunes in their own right, but a fraction of mine.

"I thought he hated me. I spent so little time with him, and when I went to see him as he was dying, he didn't recognize me at first." The memory twists in my gut.

"I'm sorry." She puts a hand on my shoulder.

"It's okay. He came out of his fog long enough to tell me to take my mother with me back to America and keep her safe. He left me everything that mattered to him. But my siblings have the only thing that used to mattered to me—a place in the official history of his life. No one knows about me out of respect for his wife. And besides taking care of my mother, keeping this secret was the only other thing he asked of me."

She wraps her arms around my neck and pulls me into a hug. She smells like the sea and coconut. "I'm sorry."

"It's fine. I loved him. It was impossible not to. But it was more the love of a citizen for their country's leader than it was a son to his father."

"Okay. But you don't have to explain yourself to me."

"I don't want you to misunderstand who I am."

"Why does it matter so much what I think?" she asks.

I don't like the question or the way she asked it.

But, it's fair. We *are* virtually strangers. It's not her fault I'm low-key obsessed with her.

"I want you to know who I am beyond what my house and money say. And maybe it's more for my mother's honor than mine, but I want to explain the comments Delé made tonight."

"Hmmm…" She smiles and nods. "How do you know him?"

"We went to boarding school together from the age of eleven."

"Wow, was that hard? Being away from home so young?"

"It was normal." I shrug. "People like our parents—his are in foreign affairs—didn't have children because they wanted a baby to cuddle and love. Children are for the propagation of a family lineage. And stay-at-home mothers weren't a thing where I'm from. Women worked and when they had children, they'd take their maternity leave, hire a nanny at the end of it, or move a retired mother-in-law in, and go back to work. My mother was no different. She loved me, but she had a life to lead separate from me."

"So, how was it? Boarding school. Fun?"

"It was…normal and what my father wanted for me."

"And now? Where do you live when you're not here?"

"I live in New York but I travel for work a lot."

"What do you do?"

"I'm in the Navy Special Forces."

"Wow. Like…a SEAL?"

"Yes. Just like that."

"No wonder your body is so perfect."

"Hardly." I scoff.

"So…shouldn't you be on a mission or something?"

"I'm on leave."

"Like vacation?

"Like, administrative."

"Oh. For bereavement?"

I wish I'd taken that when it was offered. "An error in judgment almost got my team killed. There is too much at stake to be distracted and since my father died, that's all I've been."

I shake my head slowly and open my eyes as the memories of that fateful day in Cairo come flooding back.

"That's understandable. So, if you're thinking about an MBA, does that mean you're not going back?"

I clear my suddenly dry throat. "I don't know…I need to figure that out."

"You will once you know what you really want," she says quietly. "I think I was lucky that my parents were mediocre in every way. They don't have a vision for their lives let alone mine. I've been able to forge my own path. I'm behind schedule because I had to make sure my family could stand on their own once I was gone. Now that I've done that, I can finally focus on myself."

"Why couldn't they take care of themselves?"

"No one taught them how to. And my brother is even worse and was always in debt. He's better now, but it took him hitting rock bottom and nearly us all with him to get him to stop spending money on shit he didn't need."

"And you got him out of trouble?

"Yes."

"How?"

She closes her eyes and exhales sharply. "I don't want to talk about my brother. Please. And if we were fucking tonight, I'd stay up all night, but since we're not—can we get some shut eye? I'm exhausted and have twenty-four hours of travel ahead of me."

My heart squeezes for her. And myself. I always wanted two parents at home together. But I'm grateful I had one that loved me enough to make sure I never felt alone.

I take her hand and raise it to my lips for a kiss. "You smell good."

"It's the lotion in the bathrooms at the resort." She presses her nose to my bare shoulder. "You still smell like it, too."

I nod, sorry that I let my overzealous question spook her and end our conversation before it really got started.

She's so easy to talk to. So fun, so brave. I like her.

She says she's got a man, but I don't see that as an obstacle, given what happened between us tonight.

"Sleep tight, Ms. Why."

"Yeah, Leo. You too." She yawns, rolls over and falls fast asleep in minutes.

11

Stolen

LEO

I beat the sun and wait for it to rise before I wake Cassie.

She stirs, curling her lithe body inward and then stretching, arms above her head in a huge jaw-cracking yawn. "Hey there."

"Hey yourself." I brush a kiss across her lips.

She smiles and her golden-brown skin flushes.

"Good sleep?" I brush a lock of windswept hair off her forehead.

"So good. Did you sleep at all?" She blinks up at me with the most adorably innocent expression that makes me want to tuck her back into me and never let her leave my side.

She slept like the dead and I envy her for it.

Years of being mission ready have made deep sleep a long-lost memory. The only way I sleep well is in a room with a door that can't be unlocked from the outside and with a weapon in arms reach.

And as much as I wanted to lie down next to her and sleep, it's one of the most hardwired instincts I have. Another body in my bed puts me on edge.

I kiss the top of her head. "Let's go. You have a flight to catch this afternoon and I left my house unlocked."

She springs up. "Oh my gosh, yes. Let me use the bathroom and we can head back."

* * * *

"Did we leave the lights on?" she asks as and I look at her quizzically. The boat slides into the dock next to my house and even in the low light of dawn, it looks like every light inside is on.

"I bet they can see that from space," she quips.

I chuckle because I don't want to worry her, but my blood runs cold.

Something *is* wrong.

Very.

Not only did I leave the lights off in the main residence but I have a monitoring system that tells me when they've come on.

I check my phone for notifications I know I won't find. I was distracted as fuck yesterday but a notification like that would have grabbed my attention.

But someone has definitely been here and bypassed my systems, too. Hairs stand up on the back of my neck. I need to check the resort to see who is still here and who left since last night.

"Are you okay?" she asks. I debate with myself for half a minute before I decide to just be up front with her.

"I think someone broke into the house while we were gone. I need to call the police and check to see what's missing. And, I want to get you out of here so I can take care of whatever this is."

Her face falls. "I can help you. I'm a red belt in Tae Kwon do. I can fight."

I laugh in amazement. "Wow, is there anything you can't do?"

She frowns. "Plenty. And I don't want to leave you here."

"You can't stay. Not unless you want the military police to detain and question you. They will if you're here."

Her expression changes from challenging to reluctant acceptance.

I want to kiss that pout off her lips. But I like that she doesn't jump to attention when I give an order.

"Do you have your passport and stuff?"

She lifts her purse. "Yes, I mean, my clothes are in there but it's not much."

I open my backpack and hand her and envelope. "That's $75k in cash."

She gasps and shoves it back. "No way. It was supposed to be thirty. And even that's too much."

"I'm sending you off without clothes except what's on your back. I want to make sure that if you need to, you can buy the most expensive seat on the flight out of here. Or bribe a customs officer if they give you shit."

She shakes her head. "I've never had to bribe anyone."

"You clearly haven't spent a lot of time in Africa. It's a way of life. I'll see you next week. Give me back whatever you don't use if that makes you feel better."

"Okay. If you're sure."

Her quick compliance is another tick in the pro's column.

I've stopped trying to understand why I was so drawn to her, and accepted that she's a real wild card the universe dealt me to remind me that nothing is as it seems. That even the best laid plans can change in an instant.

I don't know if there's more to how I'm feeling than the novelty of her, but I want to find out.

I glance at my watch and curse. "I need to call the police and wake up my security guys."

"They need to be fired," she says with raised eyebrows.

"Clearly." I drop into the boat's driver's seat and pull out my phone to call the helipad that's on call 24/7.

"Maurice, change of plans. I need you to come and transport my guest to Mahé now."

"Yes, boss. We're at the ready as always. Is it just her?"

"Yes."

"Okay, give us fifteen minutes to gas up and we'll be ready to take her up."

I hang up and turn back to her. "Thirty minutes."

She nods and I hate the disappointment in her eyes and that there's nothing I can do about it.

"Dammit," I curse under my breath. "My father would be livid if he knew I'd let my guard down enough for this to happen."

I can picture the outrage in his stern, bold face. And then, for a second, I am truly glad he's not here. The weight of his inexorable disappointment is something I don't miss. In the months since he died, I've realized that the only thing that made me feel like I would never measure up was the time I spent with my father and the rest of my siblings. It was a rare thing that happened twice a year at most, but the impression it left was something I would never be able to shake.

I look at Cassie, with her hair unbrushed and spilling from the pineapple-shaped bun she put it in to go to sleep, and I think I could do something different if I had someone I trusted to do it with. Someone who didn't value status over substance. The sooner she goes, the sooner I get to be done with whatever is going on here and go home. "Thank you for last night. It was the most fun I've had in a long time." I take her hand into mine.

She squeezes my fingers. "Thank you for sharing your story with me. It's given me a new perspective."

"Thank you for listening."

She smiles and looks down at herself. "I'll get the dress cleaned. Give it to you when I see you next?"

I shake my head. "Keep it. It was made for you. You look amazing."

"No. I couldn't. You've already given me all this money. You'll spoil me."

"I *want* to spoil you. Please, I insist," I add when her head shakes.

She runs her hands over her body. "Thank you. I'll treasure it."

I love the unexpected flashes of searing vulnerability she's capable of. It's so contrary to the brave face she wears and just like it did the first time I saw it, it makes my heart skip a beat.

"Give me your phone."

She hands it over and I type my number in it. I save it as Wild Card.

"Safe travels, Ms. Why." I drop a kiss on her mouth and watch until I can't see her anymore.

Whatever stroke of luck brought her into my life, it'll be worth the headache I'm about to have to deal with. Who knows what we'll end up being besides lovers? I can't wait to find out.

12

Rug Pull

LEO

The minute Cassie is gone, my entire focus turns to the crisis I'm facing.

By the time the police leave, I'm exhausted and distraught.

The ring is gone.

My heart tripped over itself when I saw that empty shelf in my mother's closet.

I'm sick to my stomach as I come down the stairs.

My phone rings and Mona's name flashes on my screen. I growl. Whatever this is, I'm going to nip it in the bud. "What's up?"

"Hey, are you alone?"

I sigh loudly.

"Jesus, Leo, I don't know why every time we talk you act like I am a complete nuisance."

"Because you are a complete nuisance. And once, it was cute. Now, it's not. So, what's up?"

"Well, I know you were surprised to see me this weekend, and I honestly was just as surprised that I wanted to be there, but you're impossible to track down."

"Why are you tracking me down? I thought you never wanted to see me again."

"Trust me, Leo, I wish I didn't have to be saying what I'm about to say." Her voice is grim. "I have to tell you something."

My blood runs cold. "What?"

"You remember that night I came over and we had sex?"

I interrupt her to stop this trip down memory lane. "Don't make it sound like that…you broke into my house and climbed on top of me when I was half asleep."

"Don't act like I did anything you didn't want. You rolled me over and fucked me, Leo, and you called me your baby when you came."

"Grow up, Mona. Men will say anything when they're coming. Why are you bringing this up? You got engaged the next day."

"I'm pregnant."

I scoff and wait for the sting of jealousy that should come.

This is the woman I thought would be my wife.

This is the woman who left me, and I'd thought my heart was broken.

But I feel nothing except relief that she is so firmly out of my grasp and that I'm finally out of hers too. "Congratulations, tell me where to send my gift."

"Mark and I have only ever used condoms. It's yours, Leo."

My knees turn to jelly. My world turns upside down.

And my plans blow away like dandelions in the wind.

13

Escape

CASSIE

"Say goodbye to paradise," the driver says as we turn into the airport's departure terminal.

"It *really* is. I can't believe I got to see it with my own eyes."

I glance to my left and gasp at the way the airport's arrival area opens up to afford me a view of the sea. I'll never get over the water here. It's dark and fathomless at night but morphs into an expanse of azure gradients the likes of which I didn't know existed in nature.

I can't believe I met Leo here.

If I hadn't made the universe a promise that this would be my last job, being here with him would have made it so. Last night, dancing with him to the beautiful music only Angelique Kijoo can make, I swore that if I could get off this island safely, I'd never do anything but what's right again.

I want to dance with him in the daylight.

I can't believe he wants to see me again for real. I want to make sure he never regrets it.

The helicopter ride was a fraction of the time of the ferry. As usual, Leo doesn't miss a detail. A car was waiting to take me to the terminal when we landed.

I'm about to enter the airport when a rough hand wraps around my bicep in a punishing grip and stops me in my tracks.

"He wants to see you," a gruff voice rumbles in my ear and I turn to try and get a glimpse of my assailant. He's dressed as a nondescript heavy—skull cap, wrap-around Ray-Bans—but I recognize Michel right away.

"Let me go, you asshole."

"You better be nice because you're in a world of trouble."

My heart is racing, but my mind is clear.

I've been practicing this for days. I made my decision. I hoped I'd get off the island without running into him, but I'm ready for this, too.

All I need is for him to believe me enough to let me get away and to ensure he has no reason to look for me when I'm gone.

I wanted this payday but I've got more than just law school, and the straight and narrow, to look forward to. I've got Leo, who's a safe place to have fun. I can't wait for more of him.

I climb into a black SUV and Michel slams the door. I stare out the mirrored privacy window between me and the front seat. The window opens a crack and a hand reaches through.

"Give me your bag," Michel says through the glass.

I smile and pass him my gigantic Louis Vuitton tote.

The window rolls back up but Michel doesn't get into the car.

Instead, the doors lock and the small window the separates the front seats from the rest of the car slides down just enough to reveal the top of a fedora-covered head sitting in the front passenger's seat.

"Who are you?" I ask.

He doesn't say a word.

I was prepared for the possibility of running into Michel. I have a plan for the for the worst- and best-case scenarios. But he's never introduced me to the people who hire us, this can't be good.

I hold my breath and wait for him to speak.

The driver's door opens and Michel climbs in. He tosses my bag through the open partition. "It's not there."

"What are you looking for?" I feign innocence and clutch my bag to my chest.

The man in the hat finally speaks. "I'm the person who instructed to Michel to retrieve the ring. Where is it?"

My heart is beating so fast, I'm scared I'm going to pass out but I don't miss a beat "I don't know. I never saw it."

"What did you do in that house for a week?" Fedora man asks.

"Slept. He was nice to me. You fired me so I didn't bother looking for that ring again."

"How do I know you didn't steal it?"

"You think I'd keep that ring and miss my huge payday? Come on. If you don't believe me, search me. Inside and out. I don't want to leave here with any doubt from you that I'm telling you the truth."

His head drops and the car is deathly quiet. If he calls my bluff I'm done.

Just when I think he's going to turn around, the door locks click open. "Get the fuck out and be grateful I'm not selling you off to compensate for my trouble. But if I ever see you again…"

"You won't." I open the door and get out of the car without another word. I don't look back to see if they're watching me, but assume they are. I rush into the airport and don't stop moving until I'm in my seat.

I don't relax until we taxi away from the gate.

I pat the stacks of cash I divided up and tucked into the one place it's always safe and undetectable—my bra. I've never seen this much money once.

Most of the people I know, including myself until recently, live on barely enough. And that's what made this job easy to do—the people I stole from had more of everything than they would ever need.

The trifles I stole helped me save my brother, get my parents out of an abyss of debt. It helped me pay a woman who cleaned my house every week, paid for college and with this final job, it would have secured the rest of my future.

I've never spent time with anyone I've been sent to steal from. And I've never thought about what the things I take have meant to the people I've stolen from.

I may have had humble beginnings, but I learn fast.

And I flew a little too close to the sun this time. I am lucky to be leaving intact.

I can't believe how badly I blew it.

And all because nothing gives me a boner like a smart man who likes to eat pussy.

I've found my weakness, and I'm not even mad about it. Because he's so much more than that. I love the hopeful way he sees the world. How hungry he is to find his place in it. And he's so kind.

I made the right choice. There will be other ways to pay for law school.

I open my purse, pull out my pot of lip gloss and press my finger into it until I find the ring.

I can't wait to give it back to him.

14

Potential

CASSIE

Ten Years Later

"I've found your future husband." Confidence sails into my office and drapes her curvy pint-sized body over the small chaise beside my window.

"Wow. Thank you. I'm so glad I don't have to look any further."

"Go ahead and laugh. Didn't I find you this office space, your house, your landscaper, and your yoga instructor? Why not?"

"Okay, so tell me all about him."

She smiles dreamily and gazes up at the ceiling. "He's perfect, Cass. He's a businessman, a veteran, a single dad with no baby mama drama, and he's one of Hayes' oldest friends. He can be aloof, but once you get to know him…he's great. He's creative, funny, and most importantly, he's hot. He's having a housewarming party and I think it's the perfect place to meet him."

"Confidence, I don't know. *His house?*"

"Yes. It's not a cave. You said you were ready. And tired of the apps. I'm telling you, this is perfect timing. He's just moved here, you're finally settled, and you're both single." She counts the points off on her fingers and grins. "What's the harm in just meeting him?"

"I don't know…I thought I was ready to dip my toe back in the pool, but now that I'm standing at the edge, I'm not sure. What if I don't like him? Or he doesn't like me. No."

She tosses her head in dismissal. "First of all, there is no way in the world he won't like you. You're the catch of the century. And, there's *no* way you're not gonna like him."

I give her a one-eyed squint. "You sound *very* sure. You know what they say—pride comes before the fall."

She flings a hand in the air, dismissing my concerns. "I know your type and he is it. At like... level 10. In every category. Trust me, Cass."

The earnest intensity of her gaze slices through my resistance. She really believes it.

"Tell me his name so I can Google him."

"Oh no, no, no." She wags a finger at me. "I don't want you to learn what anyone else thinks about him before you know what you do."

"So...he's a public figure."

She runs her fingers over lips. "I'm not saying another word. I promised Hayes."

"Why though? I mean, it's one thing to set me up. Why do I have to go in totally blind?"

"Because we know you, Cassie Mari Gold. You'll make up your mind about him before you meet him and then it'll be over before it's started."

I open my mouth to argue, but I can't argue with her because it's true. I am hypercritical of people who come into my life. "I just like to find the red flags before they're waving at me."

"That *is* a red flag."

"Fine. But it's how I've stayed safe."

"And why you're still single despite claiming you want a relationship."

"I do want a relationship. Just not at the cost of my peace of mind."

The mild irritation furrowing her brow melts and her smile is wistful. She walks around my desk and wraps her arms around me from behind, resting her chin on my shoulder and nuzzling my hair with her cheek. "I would never introduce you to anyone who I didn't think was worthy of you. And just for the record, you're like, the most perfect human—even more perfect than my icon of a husband—and there are few people who could stand next to you and truly deserve to."

I cover her hands with mine and lean into her hug. "I love the way you see me. Thank you."

She squeezes me and then stands. "Trust me, this will be the safest first date ever. You'll be there with all your new neighbors and several people you know and love. If you don't click, you can just talk to me or Dare and Beau all night."

I groan. "To save myself from being stuck at the single's end of the table with those two, I'd say yes to anything. But I would have said yes anyway. He sounds like he has potential."

She pumps the air with both fists. "Woohoo. You're gonna thank me."

"I better," I growl in mock warning.

She giggles. "If you don't, I'll go with you to Orange Theory every day for a month."

I gasp in exaggerated surprise and clutch my invisible pearls. "You *hate* Orange Theory."

"And it hates me back. I don't think it's natural to work out that hard if you're not training for something. Yes, I'm that confident. I'll pick you up at 7 p.m. on the dot. Wear something that shows off your ass." She cocks her head to the side and taps her chin.

I raise an eyebrow. "Anything else?"

"Yes. Heels. A good push up bra, something sparkly at your throat."

"In other words, dress like you?" I smirk.

She brushes a wave of her long blond locks off her shoulder and smiles like butter wouldn't melt in her mouth. "I *did* marry myself a very picky, very sexy billionaire…So, maybe listen to me?"

"I thought you weren't comfortable with being married to money?"

She shrugs. "Nothing I can do to change it and let's be real…financial security is nice, but knowing my kids will have that too, no matter what? I feel like the luckiest person on the planet. But you don't need a man for that. You've done it for yourself. And like you said, peace is priceless. No amount of money could buy the kind we're after. So believe me when I say his money is far from the greatest thing about him."

"That's good. But I don't want to dress like I'm auditioning for something…"

"It's not a bad idea to make a killer first impression on your future husband. Let him see what you're working with. Wear something special."

"I've been too busy getting out of debt to worry about my clothes."

"Let's go shopping. Let me spoil you."

A memory pops into my mind, of the last time someone said those words to me. I ended up waiting forever for it to actually happen. I'm done waiting. "Okay. You're right. But I think *I'll* spoil myself." I mutter. And show her a picture of the most beautiful dress I've ever owned.

She presses a palm to her heart, and sighs. "I love that. I have a *feeling* about the two of you.

I roll my eyes. "Confidence, every time I meet someone you're *sure* he could be the one."

She sticks her tongue out. "This is different. This time *I* picked him. And for you, I'd only pick the best. You just wait and see. I'll see you tomorrow. Look cute."

She wags a pink-tipped finger at me and saunters out.

"I'm changing the locks," I call after her.

"Don't forget to cut a spare of the new keys for me," she calls back.

I laugh and lean back in my chair, basking in the afterglow that always follows a visit from Confidence.

I was only half kidding about changing the locks.

Confidence has always had a spare key, and we walk in and out of each other's houses without knocking all the time.

Now that we work in the same suite of offices, the behavior has carried over.

And I love it and I hate it.

She's been my best friend for the last ten years and I love that we can see each other every day.

On the other hand, my productivity has taken a nose dive just when I can't afford for it to.

Adding a love interest is probably not a great idea, either, but...he sounds like everything I want in a man. Adventurous, creative, a good dad.

I'm not sure I want to get pregnant, but I like the idea of raising a young human.

And I've had a string of disappointing dates that have left me feeling like I'd be better off single. No matter what they say, every man I've met online has just wanted sex. Some are less upfront about it than others.

So I gave up on random hook-ups and let it be known that I was interested in being set up. I'm ready. And I'm horny.

I moved into my new house six months ago and I fall more in love with it every day. I love my neighborhood. I love being close to my best friend. All that's missing is someone to share all of that with.

Maybe this mystery man will be it.

15

Blind

LEO

"This space is fantastic." I turn a full circle in the center of my office and nod in approval.

"I told you so," Hayes, one of my best friends from business school, leans against the door frame. "It's perfect for you. A one-man setup. And everything you need is just a short walk away."

"It ticks every box. I love that I can walk home."

"You won't love it come May, but the drive is easy and the parking is free."

"I'll never get over that. I've never lived anywhere that parking is free."

"You've never lived in Rivers Wilde. Now that that's sorted, what do you think about my other proposition?"

I cast him a sideways glance. "Can't a man find his feet before you try to shove pussy in his face?"

He guffaws and shakes his head. "I'm telling you, that's *not* what this is."

"When it comes to the women my friends try to set me up with, that's what it *always* is. None of them can even hold a conversation. Like, don't you guys know me at all?"

Hayes crosses his arms and frowns. "I have never set you up with anyone before. Don't lump me in with your knucklehead friends who are all still single. You don't need anyone's help getting laid. I'm talking about more. She's been my wife's best friend for…" he looks up at the ceiling, "ever."

My interest piques. "You should have led with that." His wife is a rare find and has zero airs about her. "You have her picture?"

"No. But you can meet her tonight when I bring her to your housewarming."

I laugh in amazement. "You want us to have our first date at my housewarming party? With all of my friends, my mother and *Max* watching?"

He nods and smiles like it makes perfect sense. "You *love* diving headfirst into the deep end. I'm just giving you what I know you want."

I frown. "Come on. At least show me what she looks like."

"Nope. But she's gorgeous. Smart. Loves kids."

"She sounds too good to be true. But I'll take your word for it."

He slaps me on the shoulder. "You won't regret it."

"At least tell me her name."

He scoffs. "Not a chance. You run a security firm. You'd have her entire life story before I made it home. Meet her, get to know her, and make up your opinion about her that way."

"I'm just getting my feet on the ground. I've barely spent any time with my daughter."

"One night won't kill you, and Max will be there, too."

At the mention of my daughter, I tense up. "I don't know…"

"Okay, listen, if you don't like her I promise you won't have to spend the night pretending to. It's a party, there'll be other people to mingle with."

"Okay, sure. It's been a long time. Who knows what might happen?"

Maybe this will be the woman who makes me forget about the one who got away.

Max and my mother have been living here for six months without me. I've only been here twice—once since we closed on the house.

Max flew out to see me every other weekend, but it was hardly enough. I feel like I've missed so much while we're apart.

I'm very ready to settle into a routine and get to know my daughter better. And I can't think of a better place to do it.

Rivers Wilde lives up to the hype.

A deep breath fills my nostrils with the smell of coffee and comfort. Peace permeates the air in this little bubble and I've never been so glad my mother talked me into choosing Houston as the place we'd call home.

I knew very little of the city and deferred to her opinions on where we should live. This enclave in the heart of southwest Houston was the first on a very short list of places.

I didn't love the idea of a gated community—after growing up in a figurative ivory tower, it was the last thing I wanted for my daughter. But Mom promised it was nothing like that. It checked the boxes when it came to the important things like diversity, safety, good schools, and the amenities around us. Rivers Wilde feels more like a small town than a master planned community.

Since Max and Mom moved in, they've both fallen in love with their lives.

My mom said she felt like the best version of herself here. Now that I'm here, I understand what she means. Whether they've been here since the enclave broke ground in the late 1980s or are recent transplants, there's an agreement, or more like an ethos the townspeople all seem to embody—treat your neighbors as you would want to be treated.

Everyone shows up and makes an effort to keep the energy that hums through the sprawling suburb tranquil and vibrant.

I love our new house. It's grown on me. At first, I thought it looked like something out of an episode of *Real Housewives*...a modern, sleek McMansion with more windows than a house could possibly need and more space than a family could ever use.

It's very different from the two-story penthouse in New York I've called home for more than a decade. Max and my mother came to live with me a year ago and what used to feel like a lot of space proved to be completely impractical for a family. And the sounds, smells, and sights that were part of living in New York were jarring and stressful to Max.

Her mother had already moved to the other side of the world. Moving in with me was a lot, and I didn't want to change her life so much that she felt lost and didn't recognize it.

So I rearranged the stars of the galaxy that is my life, my businesses, my charities, my pet projects, and my people. And I spent the last six months transitioning to life here.

My mother has been a godsend. She and Max have always been close. There's no way in the world I would've sent Max to live without me, so I'm grateful that my mother was willing to help.

The fact that one of my best friends and his wife also live here is a bonus.

Max has friends, she loves her school, and loves the neighborhood. I love that she's happy.

I'm ready for some sort of happiness, too.

* * * *

On my walk home, I stop to get a fix of my favorite pick me up—a drink coined the green griot, full of things that taste better than they sound.

I step out of the afternoon's punishing sun and into the cool, sweet-smelling haven better known as Sweet and Lo's. The smells of sugar and yeast and butter and goodness fill the air and put me at ease instantly.

Their impressive offering of baked goods behind the glass display are mouth-watering, and the ones I've tried live up to their promise.

Maybe it's because the owners make it feel like there's love in every bite. I've only been here a week, but I already feel like a regular.

I order one of the delicious red onion and goat cheese tarts and the owner's take on chai and sit in a sunny, quiet corner of the cafe.

I'm less reluctant than I let on when I was talking to Hayes.

Am I ready to date?

Yes.

And no.

After Mona told me that she was pregnant, my whole world turned upside down. In the moment it felt crazy for so many major life changes to be happening at once.

Losing my father, taking my leave from the SEALS, becoming a father myself.

Mona's husband loves her and forgave her.

And me.

They're happily married and we coparent very well.

When I left the SEALs, I spent most of my time building my business and trying to be a present father to my daughter. I've opened restaurants, night clubs, and most recently my security company.

My former SEAL team brothers are now my business partners and it's been one of the most rewarding aspects of my life to watch them become titans of industry in their own right.

Moving to Houston, settling down and slowing down, feels like a natural progression. I'm ready for it. I want more than work. I want to be there for my daughter's recitals and milestones, and I want to come home to someone who I love spending time with.

So I'll go on this date and hope for the best.

But I'm not leaving things completely to chance, and Hayes gave me just enough information to find out who this mystery woman is without too much effort.

My mother is the neighborhood grandma. Even though she's only been here six months, everybody knows everybody and everybody knows her.

I finish my drink and head home.

The house is ablaze with light when I pull into the garage. I love it here so much. It's exactly the cookie cutter suburban life I wanted as a kid. I love that I can give this to my daughter. And after renovations and upgrades, this house is worth a cool two million. Rivers Wilde boasts of being a place where teachers and CEOs can be neighbors. I like that we can have that but also have my Sub Zero fridge, steam room, and swimming pool.

The house is quiet when I walk in.

"Mom? Max? I'm home."

"Hey baby, we're in the sun room. Come on back," my mother calls.

They're reclining on the lounge chairs, their faces draped with what looks like wet toilet paper. "Hey Daddy. Nana and I are doing our body repairs," Max says.

"Hello ladies. What are body repairs?" I drop air kisses on their foreheads and stand between their chairs looking down at them.

"We started with massages and body wraps, had our manicures and pedicures and now we're having our facials. It's our weekly self-care turned up a notch. How was your day?" my mother asks, a smile curving her lips.

There were years after my father died that her smile was rarer than a cool day in the middle of summer. I'll never take seeing it for granted. "It was good. Office lease is signed. Furniture orders are being placed as we speak."

"So glad everything is falling into place, son. Your jacket for tonight was delivered. It's in your closet."

"Thank you. So…I want to give you both a heads-up about something."

"Okay," they say in unison.

"Hayes is setting me up with someone and she's coming to the party tonight."

"Oh my god, who?" My mother sits up.

"What's setting up?"

"Like a date, Maxi," my mother says and I hold my breath.

Max pulls her mask down revealing the same wide, brown eyes as her mother. "Like a girlfriend?"

I laugh at the excitement in her voice. "Not quite. Just someone they think I'll like."

"Who is she?"

This is the opening I was waiting for. "She's Confidence Rivers' best friend. Do you know who that is?"

"Oh, you mean Cassie?"

"Is *that* her name?" This is already off to a terrible start. I won't be able to help but compare her to *my* Cassie. I haven't let myself think of her in years. She was from Houston. I wonder if she's still here. Not that it would matter. Even if she was single, she probably isn't thrilled with the guy who ghosted her.

Max squeals and jumps up to wrap her arms around my waist. "I love Cassie. She's the coolest."

My mother claps and presses her hands to her chest, peels the mask off and gets to her feet. "There *is* a god. And I knew I liked Hayes."

I smile at her and wrap my arms around my daughter to return her hug.

This is promising. "Do you have a picture of her?"

"Do I? I have several. She lives a few doors down, and your daughter loves her. She's over there all the time. She's a pretty thing, so respectful and sweet. Her mother is from Ghana, too. I hope to meet them one day." She lifts her eyebrows meaningfully. "Here." She holds out her phone.

"Lord Mom, you love to exaggerate—" The laughter dies in my throat. My heart stops. My ears ring. My breath feels hard to catch.

"See? Isn't she gorgeous?"

My head swims. "Yes, she's gorgeous."

The most gorgeous woman I've ever seen in my life.

The one I've seen in my sleep more nights than not.

The one I've never been able to forget.

The one I ghosted and let down.

The phone falls out of my hand and clatters to the ground.

My daughter picks it up, hands it to me with a heartbreaking grin on her face.

"Daddy. Ms. Cassie's my fave and she teaches the self-defense class I took when I got here. She makes the best pizza. I *love* her."

My stomach plummets and I do my best to walk steadily until I reach one of the chairs scattered around the massive, sparsely furnished living room.

The woman they were going to set me up with is the only woman in the whole wide world I would really set myself up with at this point.

My daughter, who is the magnetic core of my world, not only knows her, but loves her.

My mother likes her, and she's a little hard to win over.

"And we live on her street?"

Mom nods. "Technically, she's on our street since we've been in Rivers

Wilde longer."

I glance down at the phone and can't believe my fucking luck.

"She's been on vacation since you've been here. But she's back."

After I got the news from Mona, things felt too complicated to reach out. Life changed so fast, I could barely keep up with it and it didn't feel like a good time to bring someone into my world.

And the more time that passed, the harder reaching out became until eventually, it felt like it was too late. And pointless. Surely, she'd moved on.

I regret it more than I can say that I let her get away.

I've always told myself if I ever had a chance to apologize, I'd take it.

Back then... my life was one long shitty day. And running into her, that interlude was like being showered in the light from a million stars after living in the dark for so long. I've never forgotten how good she made me feel, how hopeful, how stimulated I was...in every way.

I'm just getting settled. Dating isn't at the top of my list, but it's on there, and I was going to prioritize it...eventually. Once I was sure my daughter was good, that my mom wasn't overwhelmed, that I could make this sprawling city feel like home.

But she's here now. And I know how fleeting time can be, how precarious our holds are on the spaces and people who make us feel good.

Here today, gone tomorrow.

That's how I found her.

That's how I lost her.

I'll never take today for granted again.

Now that I know she's single, my focus and goals shift. I'll apologize and then...I'll pursue.

"So? Leo...what do you think?" My mother nudges me.

I shoot her a smile. "Yeah, she'll do."

16

Him

CASSIE

I'd forgotten how much work getting "ready" for an evening out is.

It's not the Oscar's or anything, but it's been forever since I got my hair done, or my nails.

I twist, looking at myself in the mirror, trying to see the dress in different angles.

My five year long devotion to Orange Theory and Barre has really paid off. I'm as strong as I was in my twenties and even more agile.

This dress was a gift from him. But it's the nicest thing I own and maybe some of what I felt that night will rub off on my mystery man tonight.

I loved the way I felt when I wore it.

I loved the way he looked at me when I tried it on the first time.

I grab my splurge bottle of Baccarat and spray it on my pulse points.

There's an emotional solemnity and sense of ritual in my heart as I get ready.

As skeptical and doubtful as I've been, I hope tonight will be the beginning of something special and the end of an era that's outstayed its welcome.

The alert of my front door opening chimes. "Hello? Can I come up?" Confidence calls.

"You better!"

Her heels clack on the wooden steps leading up to the second floor.

"Are you ready?" She pokes her head around the open door of my bedroom and lets out a wolf whistle. "You look like the Cass of old." She comes to stand next to me in front of the mirror.

"And you look like Barbie's hot sister."

She runs a hand over the curve of her waist. "I have a *hot* husband to keep up with."

I roll my eyes. "Hayes thinks you're the second coming of Aphrodite when your t-shirt is stained with breastmilk and your hair smells like you use baby piss for shampoo."

She snickers. "Love conquers all."

I sigh. "If only."

"It does." She wraps her arm around my waist and pulls me into her side.

"You met your man…so it feels that way. I don't think I've ever been in love."

"All that's about to change."

We smile at each other in the mirror. We've been best friends since our first day of law school. Since then, we've been through everything and everywhere together.

But even Confidence doesn't know about my past, and what I did before I met her.

She's the most righteous person I know. Now that she's a mother, I don't think she'd accept the morally gray choices I made with much grace.

"Okay, so I talked to Hayes…and he understood how it was unfair for you to walk into a party where his friend knows everyone and you know only know us."

"And?" I wave my hand to hurry her along.

"I'm gonna show you a picture of him. No names, 'cause I don't want you to Google him on our way over."

She turns her phone around to show me the screen.

My vision goes blurry.

I blink to clear it and then wish I hadn't.

I'm slammed with so many different emotions at once. My stomach lurches.

Along with the rekindling of the hurt I felt when I never heard from him again, the disappointment, there is also panic because a part of me was afraid that the reason I never heard from him was because he'd found out what I had done somehow.

Maybe the cameras might have been working after all.

I'd want to die at the thought of him thinking I stole from him after he threw me a life line and treated me so well.

Of course, he never reached out. I stole something he loved and I lied to him more than I told the truth. I'm lucky he didn't send the police. I've wondered *why* he didn't. He never knew my real last name.

But would he call the cops now? Demand I return the ring in front of my new friends.

I just bought my dream house.

My business is taking off.

Everything is great.

The last thing I need is for him to come and blow that all up by telling everyone, including my best friend and her family, that I'm a fraud and used to be a thief.

"He's so handsome he left you speechless, right? I know. Don't tell Hayes, but he's the best-looking man I've ever seen. He's got so much swagger, you just wait till you see him walk."

My mind goes back to the safe deposit box that I opened a decade ago. I haven't touched it since; I've had no reason to visit it other than to pay the fee that keeps me able to use it.

For a minute, I consider donning my black catsuit and returning the ring the same way I took it. But those days are behind me.

I'll have to return it and tell him the truth.

Just *not* tonight.

I shake my head, hand Confidence the phone, and press my fist to my mouth. "Ugh. I'll be right back."

I rush to the bathroom and gag loudly. Lying to anyone, but especially my best friend, makes me feel like scum. But I cannot go to this party.

I flush the toilet and come out. Confidence is standing right outside the door, worry etched into her deep frown. "Are you okay?"

I lean warily against the frame of the door. "No, my stomach is fucked. I'm so sorry. I can't go with you."

She eyes me with half worry and half skepticism. "If I didn't know better, I'd think you don't think he's cute. But that's impossible." She puts a hand on my shoulder. "You rest. I'll come by after the party and make sure you're okay."

I walk her to the door and peer out the small panel window. "How did you get here? I don't see your car."

She sighs. "I guess you're going to find this out really soon so...he's your neighbor. Well, he lives two doors down."

"Two doors down?" My head spins. "That's Henny's house."

"Not that direction."

I frown. "That can't be right. It's where Anowa lives with Max."

She smiles brightly. "Oh, you know them already?"

"Wait, the man in the picture is Max's *dad?*"

"Yes. Oh my God. Please don't tell me you don't like the child."

"Are you kidding? I love her."

She frowns. "How do you know her?"

"She comes to my self-defense class and she's taken a liking to the tree swing in the back and the pizzas I make on Friday." *And me.*

Max...my heart squeezes just thinking of her. She's everything the daughter I'd resigned myself to never having would have been. "I'm going to be sick." I cover my mouth, my stomach lurching for real this time.

"Let me help you." Confidence cups my elbow with her small, but strong hand.

I shake myself loose. "No. You're already late. I'll be fine."

I won't be fine.

This is worse than I could have imagined.

I head down stairs in search of a wine glass large enough to drown my sorrows.

17

Wild Card

LEO

I crane my neck around the room searching for the top of Confidence's distinctive full metal blond head. I've always liked this part of being taller than most people. I can scope a crowd, chart my course through it and never worry that it will overwhelm me. "Where are they?" I ask Hayes when my search comes up empty-handed.

"They're on their way. Try to relax." He pats me on the shoulder as if in commiseration.

"Easy for you to say."

His wife comes into view. I look behind her, to her left and then her right.

There's no one there.

"Tesoro, I was about to send a search party," Hayes murmurs and then grabs his wife around the waist and kisses her like he didn't see her just ten minutes ago.

"I'm sorry I'm late, baby," Confidence murmurs when they break their embrace. She turns to me with a pained smile. "I'm so sorry, Leo. She wanted to come, but she got sick."

I told myself I was holding my breath in trepidation. Worried about how she'd react to seeing me and doubted that I'd feel the same connection—the one I'd hyped up in my head over the years. But now that she's not here, there's only a crushing disappointment.

I wish the party was ending rather than just getting started. "Maybe next weekend," I say.

"Are you sure she didn't show up, see his ugly mug, and leave?" Hayes says with a good-natured chuckle and slap at my shoulder.

Confidence winces. "Well...not exactly." She looks between us, chewing her lower lip.

My stomach drops. "What does that mean?"

"Yes, *what*, Tesoro?"

She winces again. "I'm sorry."

"What did you do?" Hayes narrows his eyes at his wife, then she sighs.

"I showed her a picture of him."

My stomach drops. *Shit.* She hates me.

Hayes throws his head back and groans. "Why don't you ever do what I say?"

She crosses her arms over her chest and glares at him. "Because I'm not seven years old. And she wanted to see him. She's my best friend. I thought it was a good idea."

"Glad you used past tense. Because, now look. Leo feels like a fool," Hayes says, and Confidence slaps his shoulder.

"Oh, come on. Learn to laugh at yourself, Leo. Of course you're not ugly. But Cassie's so set in her ways, she judges every book by its cover," Hayes says.

"And mine is what...lacking?"

"Oh please. You're one of the best-looking men I've ever met," Confidence says.

"I'll allow it." Hayes winks.

Confidence's eyes widen. "Leo...is it possible she knows you? She's politically active. Maybe she's heard of your dad? Maybe her mom's family are your political rivals."

"Not everyone from Ghana knows each other, Tesoro." Hayes grabs a drink from a passing server.

I forgot I'm supposed to be meeting my neighbors and welcoming them to my home.

"Actually...we kind of do. But the truth is, yes, Cassie and I know each other."

"Wait. Don't say Cassie's the one...What did you call her? Your wild card?" Hayes asks.

Confidence frowns. "Wild Card? Is that what you call her? She has it tattooed on her rib."

My dismay wanes a little. "She has a tattoo?"

"Yes. Just the words on her left rib. Is that...is that because of *you*?"

My heart squeezes at the look in Confidence eyes. "What did she tell you about it?"

"She said...it was her reminder of a dream she didn't have any more but wanted to keep alive. Or something like that..."

"Fuck." I put my drink down and run a hand over my face.

"I'm sorry. I didn't know. She didn't say." Confidence presses her palms together, distress clear in her voice and on her face.

"You didn't. It's fine."

She shakes her head, expression darkening. "No. It's not. The sight of you made her throw up. What did you *do* to her, Leo?" She crosses her arms over her chest and glares at me.

I drop my eyes. "I ended things before they could get started and ghosted her."

Confidence slaps my arm. "Leo. You didn't."

I nod, too miserable to pretend otherwise. "I've always regretted it. Never forgotten her." I glance at my watch. "Did she really throw up?"

"Yes." She purses her lips.

"Do you think I should go over there?"

"No. Not tonight. No more ambushing my best friend." She plants her feet like she's prepared to tackle me.

"It's not an ambush. I want to talk to her. Set things straight."

"Let me ask her...make sure it's cool, okay?"

"Okay." I look at her intently. "I'll wait."

She blinks. "You mean now? What about your party?"

"Dammit. I forgot."

Hayes chuckles. "Oh, Cassie's got you down bad."

I ignore him and try to corral my thoughts. Explaining them to someone else is nearly impossible. And I don't understand why she'd have such a such strong reaction to seeing me.

Yes, I ghosted her, but it's hardly as if I promised her forever first.

Maybe it's best to leave the past where it is. "Come on, let's enjoy the party. We'll try another day."

I try to do as I've instructed my guests to. But I can't. All I can think of is that she is two doors down. That she saw my picture and decided she wasn't coming. That my daughter loves her. That no matter how much she hates me, we'll still have to live next door to each other. Unless she moves because she can't stand me.

"Daddy?" A small voice next to me pulls my eyes downward.

I find myself staring into my daughter's large brown eyes. I can admit now that I didn't particularly like Mona when she told me she was pregnant. But loving my daughter, who looks so much like her mother, allowed me to see her in a different light and has allowed me to care for her, in my own way, again.

"Yes, baby?"

"I'm sleepy. I was waiting up for Ms. Cassie. Is she still coming? I can't wait for her to find out you're my dad. I'm her favorite in the class. Even though she's not supposed to have them."

She yawns and my heart expands. This child has taught me so much about life and redefined what love looks like in motion.

"You're her favorite because she's got good taste. And I promise I'm going to meet her and be on my best behavior so she'll be my friend again. But no matter what happens, I want you to remember that she's your friend, even if she's not mine—okay?"

She crosses her arms. "If she's not your friend, she won't be mine either. You're the best, Daddy. You cook me what I want, and you let me wear any color I want. You're nice, and funny, and you can fix anything."

I love the reflection she shows me of myself. And I'm glad she doesn't hold my absence from her day-to-day life against me. "Come on. Let's go get something to eat and meet the rest of our neighbors."

* * * *

"Thank you for coming." I close the door after my last guest and walk back inside to find Confidence and Max. Hayes left to take their kids home an hour ago.

"She's already asleep," Confidence sighs as I join them in my study.

She smiles down at Max, who's fast asleep on a couch in the large foyer of our house.

Just as I expected after she begged me to let her stay up even after the other kids were gone.

"Let me take her up. Thanks for hanging out with her." I stroke her head.

"It was my pleasure. I'll see myself out. Sorry about Cass. I wish—"

"Nothing to be sorry for." I press a kiss to Confidence's cheek and carry my kid upstairs.

I lay her in her bed, tuck her in, and close the door, thankful that my mother made sure the soundproofing was airtight as it has been in every house we've lived in.

My mind is back on Cassie.

I need to see her.

My mother steps into the hallway just as I'm about to head downstairs.

"Where are you going at this time of night, son?" she brushes a speck of dust only she can see off my lapel.

"To do something I should have done a long time ago." I can't put it off for another minute. I sidestep her. "I'll be back soon." *Unless things go my way.*

My life, my education, and my career have prepared me to expect the unexpected. I walk two doors down to the white craftsman-style cottage with bright blue shutters and thriving flowerbeds in the front. So, this is where she lives.

It's as alive as I remember her being all those years ago.

Last time I let her go I didn't understand the power of persuasion, of an apology, or acceptance. I walk up to her door and knock.

And I ready myself for my redemption and my reckoning.

18

Clarity

CASSIE

When my doorbell chimes, I know in my bones it's him before his face appears on my security camera.

I hit the button that unlocks my front door, take a deep, fortifying breath, and close my eyes.

He's here. It's time.

Whether it will end happily or in tears, I can't say, but the thrill of finding out—finally—where I stand with this man is a relief that I can't put a price on.

"Hello?" His voice travels through the house and up the stairs and reaches me. It carries with it memories of a former life and a longing that's never really left me.

I'm surprised to hear his footfalls on the stairs.

He's coming up. My heart races. I do my best to make my bun less disgraceful and more messy,

"Cassie?" He's in the hallway.

"In here." I call out, and hurriedly slip into my robe just before he steps into my bedroom. "Leo." His name leaves my lips on an exhale of surprise and fear.

I'm not ready.

Suddenly I want to rewind the last minute and not have buzzed him in.

What was I thinking?

His eyes burn into me with an intensity that makes me sizzle under my robe.

"Cassie." His voice is gruff.

Even if I had the words, I'd be breathing too hard to speak them.

But I don't have anything to say. Instead, I'm waiting, to see the next step in the journey I seem destined to go on with this man.

He's appeared in my life when I have room to consider sharing a part of myself freely with another human being.

Last time *he* happened, he put stars in my eyes and then yanked them out of the sky before the sun could come up.

But you stole from him.

"What are you doing here?" I hold my breath and wait for the accusation.

He shoves his hands into the pockets of his slacks and rocks back on his heels. "Why didn't you come to my party?"

We speak at once and I bite my tongue to stop myself from laughing.

He doesn't laugh, he just takes a step closer. "You're even prettier than I remember, Cassie. No. Pretty is too tame a word."

His voice is like honey and his eyes are like a black hole to somewhere I never thought I'd see. And I want to see, but I'm afraid it might kill me or hurt so much I wish it had.

I step closer to him.

What the hell am I doing?

"God, you still smell so good," he says and then closes the gap between us.

He cups my face like he has the right to. He's not mad at me. He's not calling me a thief.

He doesn't know.

I pull out of his grasp and put some space between us. "Why didn't you call me back? Or call me at all? Ever?"

He winces. "You've met my daughter? She's why. It was so complicated. And you were so right. But the time wasn't."

"So…you weren't upset with me?" I clutch the lapel of his shirt and close my eyes, trying to ground myself in the moment. It's been so long since I've felt so connected physically and safe enough to let someone else carry my weight.

He presses his nose to my temple and draws in a deep breath. "For what? Jesus, you feel good." His hands slide down the sides of my back. "So good. Just like you did then."

My body hums and I grind closer.

"God." He kisses my forehead, drags his lips down the slope of my nose and then brushes my mouth with his.

He pulls away, but keeps my face cupped in his hands. "I'm sorry I didn't make the effort then. It wasn't because you weren't worth it. I just... I didn't know how and I had her to think about. I was grieving. I didn't trust myself. I'd been impulsive and changed one life forever. I didn't...I wasn't ready."

"It's okay." My heart is in my throat as I soak him in.

I can't believe how beautiful he still is.

How good his touch feels.

How alive my body is with him next to it.

"You live two doors down?" I ask.

"You look exactly the same." He looks me up and down.

I tighten my robe and run my hands self-consciously over my hips. "I don't." I've changed so much in the last ten years. "But you do. Are you still a SEAL?"

"Once a SEAL, always a SEAL but only in my heart now." His expression grows intent. "I'm so glad I've found you again, Cassie."

I swallow down my nerves and try to return his smile. "Me, too. We need to talk."

"I'm here. Let's talk." He holds his hands out and grabs mine.

They feel so warm and familiar. And terrifyingly good. But I'm not ready for this conversation. To lose that light in his eyes when he looks at me. "I've got a really early start in the morning. Can we table it? Sorry."

He cocks his head and looks like he's going to argue. But he doesn't.

"Okay, Cass. Your call."

19

Explain

Cassie

Before I met Leo, I used to think the only thing I'd ever walk hand in hand with was struggle.

That week of stars aligning, favors being granted, touching the sun without being burned…it showed me the difference one person could make. How quickly fortunes could come and go.

How could I when he gave me the days that inspired so many of the best days of my life in the years that have followed?

I've done things and been places because I wanted to. I've let myself soak up every drop of life I can hold. I've gone to every wedding I've been invited to. I'm the friend you call when you want to take a last-minute trip to somewhere neither of us have been before.

But the thought of facing Leo this morning without the veil of alcohol that made me nostalgic makes me queasy.

We don't know each other. The fumes of the past were strong, but they weren't real.

And I've got to give him that ring.

But I need to think carefully about how.

Yet I hate keeping it from him for one more day.

The bell on the door jangles and I look up. I came in two hours later than I usually do to make sure I would miss the crowd that stopped in here for their coffee before they started work. I didn't want anyone asking how I was feeling and I didn't want to risk seeing him.

I should have known my best friend would foresee my attempt to avoid her and change her schedule to catch me out.

Confidence strides into Sweet and Lo's and walks toward me with a look of triumph and annoyance on her face. Moisture beads on her forehead, her cheeks are flushed in exertion. It's a sharp contrast to the flowery wrap dress and stiletto mules she's wearing.

"Hey, why are you sweating?" I ask.

She grabs a napkin and dabs her forehead. "I was driving by and saw you sitting here hiding, and decided to stop. The closest parking was a block over." She reaches for the glass of ice water the server just put down. "Never mind that, missy, you've got some explaining to do."

I'm tired and really not in the mood. But there's no hiding from her now. "First of all, I'm sorry I didn't tell you I knew him yesterday. Seeing him was a shock."

"What happened between you two?"

"Ten summers ago, I was working on his property in the Seychelles. I was there for a week on a job that would have earned me enough money to pay for law school. We spent a week together. Honestly, hardly even that. And I just...it's ridiculous."

A server drops the cheese danish I ordered onto the table.

"What's ridiculous?" Confidence demands as soon as she's gone.

"I don't know. We clicked. Instantly. I'd never met anyone like him. He put stars in my eyes. But we were already doomed before we said hello. Our lives were so different. That wasn't his fault. None of it was really."

"So why didn't you want to see him?"

"It's complicated."

"He's your neighbor. You can't avoid him forever."

"I know. I'm just...not ready."

She slaps the table with both hands and leans forward, her eyes wide with shock. "Well he is. The look on his face when he realized you weren't coming gave him away so quick."

I lean forward, intrigued, desperate for every glimpse of him I can get. "How did he look?"

"He was crestfallen. He tried to play it off. But he was coming out of his skin. Like he wanted to tear down the walls and get to you. "

I saw it myself last night. I just wanted to hear someone else say it.

It's been a long time since a man has looked at me the way he did yesterday.

Especially a man like him...who can have anyone. Buy anything.

And he came looking for *me*.

He's never forgotten me.

And he doesn't know I have his ring.

I drop my head into my hands and groan. "Don't get your hopes up, Confidence."

"Oh, too late for that, sister." She takes one more sip of water and then glances at her watch. "What's the problem? He's into you. You're clearly into him. Sure, back then you had different lives. But..."

I shake my head. "He doesn't know me and there's just too much water under that bridge for me to go back."

"No there's not. Not if you think there's a chance. Hayes told me Leo said you're the one who got away, Cassie. He's never stopped thinking about you. Why can't you give him a chance?"

Confidence looks so happy. I hate myself for erasing that smile off her face, but I have to tell her. I take a deep breath and just say it.

"Because I stole from him, Confidence."

Her gasp is audible, my cheese danish that she'd just taken a bite of seems to get lodged. She makes a weird hacking noise and points to her throat.

"Oh my God," I stand behind her and slap her back until she starts coughing. She grabs her glass of water and takes a huge swallow, throwing her head back to deep breathe. She sighs and then looks back at me, her eyes wide. "What do you mean, you *stole* from him?" She shakes her head. "Cassie, you're not a thief. How is that even possible?"

"Before I met you, my brother got himself into some financial trouble. I got him out of it by stealing something to satisfy a debt. I was a gymnast. I was athletic and I was very good at blending in. "

She pinches her nose. "No, you're not."

"I *was*. Anyway, I did it. It was easy. It was good money I got my family out of debt."

She shakes head, her eyes wide. "Why didn't you tell me?"

"By the time I met you, I'd paid it all off. I wanted to put it behind me and I didn't think you'd understand."

"I do understand. I can't say I wouldn't have done the same. Anyway, go on." She rests her chin on her propped-up hands like a child eagerly awaiting their favorite bedtime story.

"When I got into law school, I decided it was time to stop. But, I got a call about a job with a payday so big, it would pay my tuition for all three years. All the other jobs I'd done had been for other people. This was for *me*. All I had to do was join the staff of a private resort in the Seychelles. Find my way into the home on the same property and find a ring. Except, it wasn't just a ring. And Leo...wasn't just a mark. I took the ring because I was sure the people who sent me would send someone else after me to finish the job."

She covers her mouth with both hands, her eyes wide with shock.

"I wanted to keep it safe. I thought I'd see him in a month, max. I hope you know I'd never steal from you or anyone I loved today. I swear," I plead, humiliated that I'm having to say this.

She drops her hands and reaches across the table for mine. "Of course I know that. I'm sure Leo will, too."

"I'm not sure." I shake my head miserably.

"Tell him and see."

The thought makes my stomach lurch. "I would give back every penny I ever took to go back and have a real chance with Leo."

"You have a chance now."

"Do you really think he'll understand?"

"Someone once told me that we're all a product of our environment. That we can't help some of the choices we make because we're hardwired. That forgiveness is for us as much as it is for the people who hurt us." Confidence puts her face just a couple of inches from mine. "Sound familiar?"

"No. It sounds naive. How can he forgive me? I'm the reason he's been without this thing that means so much to him."

"He may be upset, but I think Leo is a smart man, and he'll understand and forgive you, too. You were trying to make amends. You have really turned your life around," she says and squeezes my hand. "And it's time to forgive yourself."

20

Serendipity

Cassie

"Twice in one day, how'd I get so lucky?" I blow a kiss at Confidence through the screen of my phone.

She mimes catching it. "Just checking on you." She peers into the screen. "Are you in the *produce* section?"

"Yup. Trying to figure out what to cook tonight."

"Why are you pretending you're going to eat any of that stuff in front of you when we all know the *only* thing you can cook is that pizza?"

I stick my tongue out at her. "I'm not in the mood for pizza and the only thing worse than whatever I'll find to whip up is how hungry I am."

"You're in Rivers Wilde for real now. There's not a restaurant here that doesn't serve banging food. You should go to The Market, you'll pay a tiny mark-up for the semi prepared food there."

"I'll take a look around, figure it out. Where are you?"

"At Twist, getting dinner for the kids. I didn't feel like being a short-order cook tonight. Come join us if you want."

"Maybe tomorrow. I'm pooped."

"Okay, Cass. Our food is here, gotta go. Love you."

"You, too." I hang up regretting my decision not to join them.

I'm tired of eating alone. I don't like living alone. I don't like traveling alone. I don't like sleeping alone.

I'm tired of hearing my friends who are happily coupled up acting like they know what it's like to be alone. Or saying that I should relish all the nights I get to go to bed all by myself and get to watch what I want and not worry what anyone else wants to eat.

More than anything, I'm sick of being made to feel like there's something wrong with wanting to be in a relationship more than I want to have it "all".

I've learned to give myself the hugs I need. But... every time anyone hugs me, I realize how absent affection and intimacy are from my life.

I thought I'd finished paying my dues, and now it seems to be all I'm destined to do. The only man I want is about to find out I lied to him and deprived him of something that means a lot to him.

"Hey Cassie," Ju-won, the cashier whose line I always get into, waves at me as I grab a basket.

I've been shopping here for years. Even when owning my own home in Rivers Wilde was just an item on my vision board, I've treated the enclave like home. I got my hair braided here, my nails done, taught self-defense, worked out in the gym. And grocery shopped. I love the consistently bright, reassuringly abundant displays of fruit that change seasonally.

I grab a container of fresh cut mango, a bundle of grapes, and head to the bakery.

A baguette smothered in butter sounds like the perfect meal that will require very little effort and will soak up all the wine I intend to consume during my pity party tonight.

"Hey, Ms. Gold, wait up."

I turn with a smile already on my face. "Hey Jason." I wave at the young man who works as a stocker.

"I saved one for you. I know you like 'em." He holds out a container full of coconut chunks.

"Oh my God, you might have just turned my whole day around. Thank you." I clutch the container of coconut to my chest. It's my favorite. The thought of that for dessert makes the prospect of eating alone a little less sad.

I would hate to have to share this.

"Enjoy."

"Cassie!" The initial burst of pleasure at the sound of little Max's voice fizzles out when I find myself face-to-face with her father. He looks good enough to climb. His long muscular legs would stop traffic, thank God for the thigh muscle loving inventors of soccer uniforms.

"Hey there, Ms. Why."

The space between us pulses with energy that makes me want to get closer to him. But first, I have to explain.

"Hi, Leo."

Max runs between us and wraps her arms around my waist. "I missed you. Are you making pizza this Friday?"

"I sure am."

"Yay." She hugs me tightly and for just a moment, the knot of worry in my stomach loosens. I hug her back.

"Max, you shouldn't just invite yourself over to dinner," her father chides.

"She's got an open invitation," I say with a smile down at the little girl.

Her smile is so open and trusting. I hope she'll still look at me like that once I tell Leo the truth.

I should bid them good night, but I don't want this moment to end. "Anyway, what are y'all up to?"

"Daddy is making his famous shrimp and spaghetti and a salad with my favorite salad dressing for dinner tonight. I haven't had it in forever and I begged him."

"She hardly had to beg. As if I ever say no to you Maxi-girl."

My heart melts.

His smile is tentative, and I feel so guilty that somehow he thinks he's done something wrong. That he has something to apologize for.

His mother walks around and gives me a hug as well. "Cassie, if you're free you should join us for dinner. We have plenty of food that's not pizza."

I flush. "My cooking repertoire is short, but quality over quantity, right?"

"Good thing your neighbors know how to cook and like your company," Leo says. "You could eat with us every day if you wanted."

I laugh, as if amused and not alarmed and excited by the prospect of eating with them. "Let's just start with tonight. You might change your mind about that when you see how much I eat."

"Nothing could change my mind."

I smile, but the latte I had for lunch curdles in my stomach. "Okay, thank you for the invite. I'd love to."

21

First Cut

LEO

"Ouch, shit." I press my finger into my mouth and suck the nicked tip.

I can't keep my eyes on the chopping board when Cassie is sitting in the same room as me.

And even though I wish she'd meet my eye, the view I'm being afforded is nothing to sneeze at.

It's the first time seeing her and Max interacting. They're as thick as thieves with their heads bent over a pile of glass beads my mother brought from Accra.

I'm almost done so I pick up the chopping board and toss the onions, squash, tomatoes, snap peas, and mushrooms all into the huge wok.

Then I pick up a head of purple cabbage and take out my mandolin to start slicing.

"This one's for you, Ms. Cassie." Max holds up a string of blue and red beads.

"Oh honey, thank you. I love it."

"I love yours too."

"Actually, I made it for your dad," Cassie's words, though spoken casually, pull my eyes back to them.

"For me?"

"Yes. To say I'm glad we connected again. Thanks for reminding me that wild cards are real."

My whole body lights up. Maybe there's hope after all.

"I don't know what to say…but thank—ow!" I yank my hand back from the mandolin and yelp at the sting of pain coming from the top of my finger. "Oh shit."

I run my hand under the cold tap and wince at the sting of water hitting my hand. It's only then that I see how deep the cut is. My blood runs cold.

"Oh my god," I whisper. Blood pours from what used to be the tip of my thumb.

"Are you okay?" my mother asks as she strolls into the kitchen.

"Daddy cut himself."

"Leo, what's wrong with you? You never cut yourself in the kitchen."

"I don't know." I grab a towel and wrap it around my hand.

"Let me see."

Cassie slips off the stool. "Leo. Are you okay?"

The concern on her face is gratifying, but the horror that replaces it when her eyes drop to my hand brings me back down to earth. "Leo, this is bleeding pretty badly."

My mother wraps a towel around my hand. "Ouch." I push through the pain and wrap it even tighter. "Just need to apply pressure."

I press down on my thumb and pain shoots all the way up my arm. "Shit."

"Oh no. You're bleeding. A lot."

"It's fine. It's just a cut," I say and then look down and almost scream. It looks like a murder scene. The towel is soaked through. "I can't stand the sight of blood."

"Okay, Max and Anowa, you take his left side. I'll take the right."

Their shoulders press into both sides of me.

"I can walk," I grumble and stiffen —only to sway and nearly fall on my face.

"I've got him. Come on, ladies." Cassie's voice sounds so far away.

"Blood makes him faint," my mother says in a hushed whisper.

"That's not true," I protest.

"The urgent care is eight minutes away. I'm driving," Cassie says.

"Why is it so dark outside?" I ask.

"I think he's in shock." I hear my mother's voice from far away.

I close my eyes. "I'm just tired."

"Okay. You rest. We'll take care of you," Cassie whispers in my ear.

They are the last words I hear before I pass out.

22

Now

LEO

I cross the lantern-lit path from my door to the sidewalk that connects my house to Cassie's.

I hold my breath and knock before I lose my nerve.

The small intercom next to the door buzzes. "Leo?"

I look up and into the small camera installed by her front door. "I hope it's alright that I stopped by."

"Hold on."

It takes her a full two minutes to come to the door.

Her hair is caught in a towel and she's wrapped in a fluffy sky-blue robe. "I was in the bath."

"I can come back." *Or I could join you.*

She shakes her head. "No. Come in." She stands aside and I slip in beside her.

Her house is as bold and warm as she is. The other night I rushed straight into her bedroom and missed the wall-sized paintings and elegant sculpture art that adorns the room.

I can't wait to really explore them.

"Is everything okay?" she asks and I turn my attention back to her.

We face each other in the foyer. "Yes. I just wanted to say thanks for last night."

She shrugs. "It's fine. How's your thumb?"

"Still here, thanks to you." I wave my bandaged hand between us.

"You did a number on yourself. The doctor said it would take months to heal."

"And that I'll have a new thumbprint when it does."

"I can't believe you were using the mandolin without gloves."

"I can't believe you were sitting in my kitchen. Laughing with my daughter. Talking to my mom. Looking good enough to eat yourself," I blurt out.

She clutches her robe closed and squares her shoulders. "You're very direct."

"I learned the hard way about waiting for the right moment to say how you feel. And Cassie, you should know that I have fantasized about this scene for years."

"For *years?*" She gives a skeptical frown. I smile to see it.

"They have felt like eons. I was sure you'd have moved on. Certain I'd lost my chance. But I did what I thought was best for Max."

She smiles at me. "She's amazing."

The love on her face when she speaks about my daughter nearly does me in. My determination to get her to give us a chance amplifies.

"She is. I want her to know her life is hers to direct. I was an extension of my father's dreams until he died. I didn't start making my own choices until it was almost too late. I want her to have as much say in her life as I can give her. And all the choices I've made since then have centered around her. But now..." I sigh and look up at the ceiling.

"Now?"

"She still needs me, but Max is choosing the people she wants to be close to and I want her to have other relationships besides me and her grandmother. With her attention elsewhere, I'm ready to think about my life again."

"And when you think about your life, what do you want?"

"I've *got* everything I want. Except you."

Her chest heaves and her eyes grow wide.

"Are you surprised?" I ask.

"Yes. No. I mean—I think you're letting nostalgia cloud your judgement."

"No, I'm letting the present cloud my nostalgia. I remembered a rebellious wild child who didn't want kids or domesticity. I'm not sure I would have trusted her with my kid."

"And now that I'm a lawyer, you do?"

"No, now that I've seen the life you've built, the way you love the people around you, yes, I trust you with her."

Her eyes glimmer with something that looks like "yes." But she still shakes her head.

I sigh, heavily. "Let me kiss you. Kiss me back. Let me make you come and then, let me fuck you. Whatever comes after that— those are things we can agree we both want. Please," I implore, holding her eyes and letting her see my desperation. I don't care about my pride. I just need to know where we stand.

Her eyes soften and she runs a hand through her thick hair. "Your mother is expecting you back."

"She's not." I wink at her.

She purses her lips. "Why won't you just let it be?"

"How can you expect me to do that when you look at me the way you do? When I hear that sexy whimper of yours, every time I close my eyes." I stroke a hand down her cheek and she sighs.

I slide my hands along the slope of her shoulders, over her slim back and pull her into me. Her body is warm and soft and fits against mine like it was made to.

"You still smell so good, Leo," she whispers into my chest. Her small hands are pressed to either side of my heart.

"So do you."

"I just took a shower. I still need to put lotion on."

"I can help you with that." My groin tightens, my shoulders loosen, and blood starts to travel south and away from my brain.

I slip a hand between us and untie the belt of her robe and let my hands fall to my sides. "Let me see you."

She takes a step back, her dark eyes wide and locked on mine. She licks her lips, swallows and nods.

"I shouldn't," she says as she fingers the lapel of her robe.

My mouth waters. "But you will anyway. Because you want me as much as I want you."

"I do." She nods and then rolls her shoulders until the fabric slips from them and flutters to the floor. My heart skips a beat and my vision tunnels so all I see is her.

She is even more beautiful than I remember.

Her skin is so smooth it glistens. Her body is lithe, elegantly muscled and soft at the same time.

Her breasts are fuller than they were ten years ago and my dick goes rock hard at the sight of her large dark brown nipples already standing at attention. The tattoo that Confidence told me about is visible just below the swell of her left breast.

She cups her breast and tugs the plump stiff peak. "What do you think?"

"Cassie, I—" I clear my throat and step forward as all the blood in my body rushes to my dick. "Oh, you'll do. Nicely." I say before my mind shuts down and I only know one thing— need.

I close the gap between us with a long stride and pull my shirt over my head in one swift movement. I wrap an arm around her waist, my hand spanning her narrow back. Desperate for the contact again, I pull her flush against me.

There's a moment of clarity in the relief the contact brings.

This is right.

She is right.

There's *something* here, physically and emotionally. And I want to pursue it. "Can I stay the night?"

Her eyes cool and her lids droop a little, as if my words have hypnotized her.

She sways forward, bringing her head toward me. "You just *try* to leave. I'd fight to stop you."

I reach up, cup the back of her neck and bring her close enough for me to nip her sweet mouth.

No matter how many times I kiss her, I'll never get over how good she tastes, how naturally we move together.

The nips turn into tugs and then our lips are dueling.

I walk us backward until we hit a chair. She grips my biceps, turns me around and pushes me into it.

"Hi there, handsome." She grins down at me and licks her lower lip. "Here let me help you, out." She kneels between my thighs and unbuckles my belt, unfastens my pants and hooks her thumbs at the waist. "Lift up," she whispers.

I tilt my hips so she can pull my pants down and off. My dick is fully erect and bobs against my stomach. "Thank you universe," she presses her hands together and tilts her head up in a mock prayer and then grins down at me. "Oh, this is going to so worth the wait." She licks her lips and I have to stop myself from fisting her hair so I can direct her mouth to my cock.

I grab my dick to take the edge off my desperate need for friction. "Are you just going to look at it?"

"It's so beautiful, I could." She gets to her feet and straddles me, connecting us skin to skin from thigh to chest.

She wraps her arms around my shoulders and rocks her hips until I'm nestled in her warm heat. Her nipples are dragging down my chest, so stiff, that they send shivers through me. I run my hands down her naked back, not breaking the kiss while I use the tip of my dick to massage her clit.

I catch her whimpers on my tongue, use them as fuel and direction as I take her up.

My fingers tangle in her braids and I hold her head in place while I feast on her.

I could come just from kissing her—her mouth is soft, so warm, so sweet.

But I'm desperate to taste the rest of her, too. I trail kisses down the fragrant soft column of her throat and nuzzle her collar, dragging my tongue along the slope of her breast and tracing her nipple with the tip of it.

"Leo, oh yes," she gasps.

Her hands cup my head hard as I suck her sensitive peak into my mouth. I reach between us, and slip my fingers between her slick lips, find her clit and stroke it.

I release her nipple on a groan. "You're so wet already Cassie, baby."

"You made me this way," she sighs and rolls her hips.

I rub small circles, watching her face, entranced by the way her mouth falls open, the way her lashes flutter when she closes her eyes, the way her nostrils flare when I slip my finger inside her.

Her cunt contracts around me, grasping and hungry and ready for me. I want inside her so badly but I'm not ready for this to be over. I already know I'm not going to last long. Not tonight. I want to make sure she gets off good before I do.

I slip a second finger inside her. She's so tight but slick.

"Leo, I need more." She draws in three sharp breaths and a bed of sweat runs down her chest between her breasts.

"Tell me what you need. Tell me and I'll give it to you."

"I want you to suck my nipples."

"And then?"

"I want to ride your hand until I come."

My mouth leaves hers and I press hot, open-mouthed kisses down her neck, sucking hard and deep as I make my way to the thing I'm really after. I nip the succulent peak of her breast before I take it back into my mouth.

We groan in unison at the swell of it against my tongue.

I slip another finger inside her and watch in wonder as she bites down on her lower lip and drops her head onto my shoulder. She lifts her hips and pulls my hand back and up again so that when she lowers herself again, my fingers enter her with a thrust. I curl them and find her spot and stroke while she gets herself off.

"Ugh, Leo. I'm coming. God." Her head falls back and she arches her back as she comes with a wail that nearly takes me over with her.

But I reign myself in. I'm not ready to be done.

I hold her through her climax. When she's caught her breath, she lifts her chest off of mine and presses a wet kiss to my lips.

She wiggles out of my hold before I can deepen it. "Come here," I growl when she hops off my lap. I grab her by the wrists and pull her back to me.

"Patience, it's my turn." She pulls her hands free and gets to her knees again. "Finally, we are reunited," she says her eyes trained on my throbbing erection. "I've missed you." She wraps her small warm hand around it.

She gives it two quick strokes. "It's fucking hot seeing you with my dick in your hand, Cassie." I grunt.

"Oh, it's about to get even hotter," she quips.

Before I can catch my next breath, my dick is in her mouth. I slip my hands into her hair, clenching handfuls of it, and guide her up and down.

I want to be gentle with her, but the sight of her dark hair cloaking my thighs as she moves up and down on me is too much.

My hips move faster and she gags when the head of my dick hits the back of her throat. She groans and pulls away.

"Is it too much?" I ask.

"Never." She moves to her knees, lifting herself up before she lowers her head and takes me back into her mouth. She cups my ass taking me all the way in. Her throat is relaxed and when the tip of my dick hits the back of it, I almost black out.

It's the most perfect place on Earth.

Nothing has ever felt so good as she does right now.

"God you're such a good girl Cassie, so good."

She looks up at me, her eyes glassy with the tears spilling down her cheeks. Seeing this strong woman on her knees pleasuring me sends me over the edge too.

My balls tighten in warning, but I can't it hold back. The current starts in the soles of my feet and speeds up my legs and through my hips. I try to pull her off me, to warn her.

"I'm going to come." I release her head but she doesn't ease up. And when I come harder than I have in my life, she doesn't stop until I do. My fingers thread through her hair and the feel of the silky waves slipping through my fingers helps my heart to slow and my breathing to even out.

She lets me slip from her mouth and gazes up at me through her thick lashes, her golden eyes glowing through them. A proud, roguish smile is on her lips as she stands up.

My hand goes to cup her face. I gaze down into her eyes and say the first thing that comes into my head. "Can I fuck you now?"

She grins. "Yes. You can."

I pick her up, carry her upstairs, lie her on the bed, and strip out of the rest of my clothes while she watches.

"You are so beautiful, Leo." She runs a hand down my chest when I join her on the bed, lay next to her and drape her leg over my hip.

"I've been waiting for this for so long, I can't believe we're here."

She cups my face, leans forward and kisses me. "Believe it."

I find her with my fingers first, make sure she's as wet as she was before and groan when her sweet honey runs down my hand. "Put me in."

Her eyes on mine, she reaches between us and wraps her hands around my erection and guides me home. She's tight but giving, hot and soothing all at once.

"This is so perfect, baby," she whispers through barely parted lips.

I thrust up slowly at first, getting used to the feel of her, trying to make it last. But it's too good and too sweet and I pump my hips faster every time I pull out.

"Hold on to me, Cassie," I command. Her arms and legs wrap around me in a vice grip.

I wrap my arms around her and drive into her. We kiss while we fuck and when she comes, I catch her cries on my tongue. Then I chase my own release and finally, after years of waiting, make the woman of my dreams mine.

23

Wrecked

CASSIE

I'm ruined. Absolutely wrecked. Leo climbs off me, the air instantly cooling my sweat slick skin. "I'll get us a towel to clean up."

I close my eyes. I should be so happy right now but as satisfied as my body is, my heart is restless. I have to tell him.

Now.

Even if it hurts.

Even if he leaves.

I can't kiss him again with this lie between us.

He comes out of the bathroom, towel in hand, smiling like he just got an award. Until he sees my face.

"What is it?"

I sit up. "Leo, we—"

The doorbell rings and we both freeze. "Who is that?" he asks and goes over to the window.

I grab my phone to look at the screen.

"It's your mom," I say and look at him wide-eyed.

"Max," he breathes. He slips on his pants and runs out of the room without another word. My heart is in my throat as I pull on my robe. I grab his shirt and belt and walk down to join them holding my breath, praying that everything is okay with Max.

"You scared the shit out of me," he's saying to his mother as I reach the bottom of the stairs.

"What's happened?" I join them in the foyer, pulling my robe tight.

Anowa's normally peaceful expression is twisted with dismay. Her eyes are wide with worry. "I'm so sorry, Cassie. Leo's brother just arrived, unannounced. I didn't know what to do."

"Your brother?" I look up at Leo, confused.

"Bismark." He closes his eyes briefly.

"Did you know he was coming, Leo?" his mother asks.

He sighs. "Of course not, mama. I would have told you. I'll be right over. I just need to get dressed."

24

Foiled

CASSIE

"Today is the day you're going to tell him." I chastise the weak, wanton women staring back at me in the mirror. I hold her gaze and turn my phone over in my hand. "I *have* to do it. And first thing."

The phone vibrates in my palm and I drop it. "Get it together, Gold."

Leo's name flashes on it and my panic spikes but I answer anyway. "Hey. I was just about to call you and see if could come over."

"Sorry, Ms. Why, change of plans. My brother wants me to attend an event with him tonight."

"Oh. Okay. No worries."

"I'm sorry. He rarely asks anything of me. Can you join us for dinner tomorrow, though? I'd love for you to meet him."

"Sure. But—"

"But?"

"Nothing." *This is the worst.* But I can't tell him over the phone. "I'll see you tomorrow. What time were you thinking?"

"Is 6 p.m. too early?"

"No." I hope it's not too *late*. "It's perfect. I'll see you then." I hang up and crumple into a heap on the floor.

I'm sick of carrying this monkey on my back. I've lived with it for ten years—one more day shouldn't feel unbearable. But it does.

25

Suspicion

LEO

"So what took you to the Seychelles?" Biz leans back and eyes Cassie up and down.

Cassie has been on edge all night. She's good at hiding it but I can tell her laugh is a little flat, her smile just short of being true and she's fidgeting with her ring as she did when I met her all those summers ago.

But my brother's demeanor has me on edge too. I don't understand why or how, but there's something disconcerting in his expression every time he looks at her.

Cassie darts a look at me that I think is a cry for help.

"She said it already, Biz. She was there for work. What is this?"

"It's okay, Leo." She puts a hand over mine.

"Isn't that the weekend the house was broken into?" he asks me.

I sit up fully then.

"How do you know that? I never told you."

He looks at me with disdain. "I'm our nation's most senior intelligence officer. How do you *think* I know? I also know the only person on that island we couldn't account for was her."

"She was with me and away from the house when the break-in happened. What did she need to account for?"

"Your home was broken into. Nothing was taken but we investigated anyway. The background check in her employment file had no supporting documents."

I clear my throat. I have never told him what happened to the ring. He never asked and I just…I couldn't. "Right."

Cassie shoots to her feet. "I was a last-minute hire. Er… Can I talk to you in the kitchen, Leo?" she asks and she strides out of the room before I can answer.

"I'll be right back, Biz."

My brother nods and I follow her into the kitchen. "What's going on Cassie?"

"This is terrible timing, but I have to tell you why I was really there that week."

* * * *

When she's finished, I'm numb.

"So, you came there to steal from me and then used your misfortune, my kindness, to see your mission through?"

"No. I only took it to make sure no one else did. I thought I'd see you again. In a week. I was keeping it safe. I swear."

I shake my head in disbelief. "Where is it now?"

"In my safe deposit box. I can get. Right now."

"No. Right *now*, I just need you to leave, Cassie. I need to think about what you're telling me."

"I'm sorry, Leo." She presses her palms to the kitchen counter.

"Good night. You can use this door. I don't want my brother to know he was right." I turn my back on her and don't turn around again until the back door slams closed behind her.

I walk back into the living room.

Biz gets to his feet.

"I just heard from my head of security. He said he heard rumors that she was a thief."

I stagger back. I'm shocked, heartsick, confused. And worried for Cassie. Is she going to be in trouble? "What kind of rumors?"

"From the other staff. That things disappeared in places where she'd worked before."

I sigh and sit. "It was a long time ago. She didn't actually steal from me."

I can't believe I'm defending her. But it's true. She took the ring intending to give it back.

"I'm sorry. I could tell you liked her. But denial is no good."

"She has the ring."

My brother stops pacing and turns to face me. "What do you mean?

What ring?"

"Dad's ring. She has it. She says she took it that night for safekeeping. That she always planned to give it back."

His eyes narrow at me. "You mean you haven't had the ring all this time?"

I force myself to meet his gaze. "I haven't. I didn't want to tell you."

"Why not? I'm your brother."

I could drown in the guilt and frustration I feel. "And there's your answer. That ring should have been yours. I knew it then, but he gave it to me."

He shakes he head. "Leo. He gave it to you because he loved you and wanted you to know. But if you'd told me it was missing, I would have helped you look for it. Found out about her sooner."

"She didn't steal it and she's giving it back. She even offered to go get it right now."

His eyes bug out. "So why didn't she?"

"Because I just found out she lied to me. I asked her to leave. I need some space to think."

"You need to call the police."

I freeze. "No. I don't. I'm not sure what will become of us, but I am certain I'm not calling the authorities on her. And neither are you."

He grinds his teeth together. "You have been in this country too long. You've gone completely soft. But she's pretty. I understand."

She's so much more than that. I exhale sharply, eager to stop talking about this with him.

"Okay, enough of that. Tell me what really brought you to town."

He doesn't say anything, his expression is unreadable and I know he's going to push back.

"Fine. I came to town for the event yesterday. I'm staying because I want to spend time with my brother who I never see."

I push Cassie to the back of my mind and smile. "How long are you staying?"

He smiles and hooks an arm around my shoulder. "Just a few days. Give us a chance to catch up and spend time with my niece. I'd like to see your life here in America. Maybe convince you to give Ghana a chance."

I shake my head and laugh, but it's stilted.

A few days can't hurt, and I do need time to think.

And Cassie does, too.

26

Mea Culpa

Cassie

It's after midnight when my phone rings. I'm already awake. I've been waiting for his call. But now that it's here, I'm not sure what to say to him.
If I'm prepared for what he's calling to say to *me*.
It's been two days since I told him.
I sent breakfast to his office the next day and texted to wish him luck on a meeting I know is important to him.
I went to the safe deposit box the next morning. I almost left the ring in his mailbox but I was afraid it would go missing again and then I'd really be up shit's creek.
I expected this reaction from him. Welcomed it, even.
If he's upset it means he cares.
If he cares maybe he'll want to forgive me. Maybe even understand.
But I'm also prepared for the worst. I'm having my parents over for the first time tonight and I hoped he'd be here.
The last time I lost him, it hurt. But nothing like how I feel just thinking that he might not find it in him to get over this.
"Cassie, I called to say—"
"I'm sorry, Leo. I'm so sorry. You've already had to do so much "understanding" in your life. I wouldn't blame you for not wanting to be in a relationship with someone who asks you to do it again. But I swear that was the last time I was ever dishonest. I know I have no right to ask you to forgive me but I-"
"Cassie, enough. We need to do this face to face."

27

Twist

Leo

I brought Biz here to have a beer and talk before he left for the airport. Max and Mama went to see *The Little Mermaid*.

"It's been so good to see you, Biz."

"Thank you for letting me intrude." We clink beers and take a sip.

The cold, bitter bite of foam is usually my favorite part of this drink, but tonight I barely taste it. I can't stop thinking about Cassie. I can't wait to see her.

Biz reaches across the table and places a hand on my shoulder. "I'm sorry your young lady turned out to be a thief."

I flinch at the word. "She's not a thief."

"She is. And the sooner you see it, the better. She still hasn't given you the ring back."

I close my eyes and run a hand over my head. "She's tried. It's at her house. I'm going to get it tonight. And talk to her."

His head jerks back a bit. "Tonight?"

"Yes."

"Let me go for you."

I choke on my sip of beer. "Why would I do that? And don't you have a flight to catch?"

He frowns and then shrugs. "Never mind. I thought I'd save you from seeing her."

"I want to see her. I'm falling for her and I care about her deeply."

He sighs. "You are so much like him."

I cock my head to the side. "What do you mean?"

"Love. You think it's more important than anything." He sneers and I'm taken aback. I've never seen the expression he's wearing now and it makes my blood run cold.

"What does that mean?"

"Nothing." He drops his head and when he looks back up, his expression is softened and he's smiling. "I'm sorry. I think I'm overcompensating for the time I wasn't there for you. You're an adult and you don't need my advice. I'm sorry, Leo."

My mood has whiplash. "It's okay, Biz."

He nods. "Thank you. I need to use the facilities, excuse me."

As soon as he's gone, I relax in my seat and replay our conversation.

Something is off.

One of the promises I made to myself when I moved to Houston was that I would listen to my instincts and not allow fear or duty to make my choices again.

I've spent the last few days doing the opposite and I'm coming out of my skin.

I have a lot of respect for my brother. He's the only one of my half siblings who even acknowledges my existence.

Our relationship is important to me. Besides Mama and Max, he's the only family I have. We speak frequently, but I haven't seen him in years. His mother still doesn't like the fact that I exist and so he's kept his distance.

I should be happy he's here. But instead, I feel...irritated.

I used to stop everything when they called. Asked, "how high," when they said jump. All in the hopes that one day, they would bring me into the fold.

And then I had Max. And I realized that blood isn't thicker than water. Love is a *choice*. Nothing I did could make them choose to love me. Because they didn't want to.

And since I stopped chasing them, I only hear from him when he needs something. So his whole "just called to say I love you" act rings false.

He slides back into the booth a few minutes later. "Are you ready to head out?" I ask as soon as he sits down.

"Well, actually—"

"Leo!" Confidence's voice carries over the low din in Twists' large dining room. She's with the kids.

"Hey, y'all," she greets us as she approaches, her smile wide and welcoming. "Hey Biz. I didn't realize you were still here."

"I'm leaving tonight," he says in a clipped, decidedly unfriendly tone.

Her smile disappears and I look at him like he's grown two heads.

"Okay. We're here for dinner and the kids are starving so we'll see you later."

She gives me a wide-eyed look and mouths WTF as she turns to leave.

"Biz, what was that?"

"What was what?"

"You were rude."

"She interrupted me."

"She didn't know that and this is our neighborhood watering hole, people say hello."

"Fine. Sorry. And what I was *trying* to say is that I just heard from my driver. He's been delayed. I need a ride to the airport."

"I'm going to see Cassie tonight."

"She'll be there after my flight leaves," Biz, says. "I was really hoping we could continue our conversation. One second, please." He pulls out his phone and sends a text. "So you see, I am going to need you to take me."

"I can't."

"Leo—"

I slap my palm on the table. "Biz. Stop. I'm not the most important person in your life, you aren't the most important in mine. It's been great to see you. But I have to go. Your car will be here soon."

"Wait." He grabs my arm to keep me from leaving.

"What?"

He looks at me intently but doesn't say anything.

"Biz? What's up?"

He lips twist in a bitter smile and he lets me go. "Nothing. What will be, will be."

"Okay," I say.

"If you could please take me back to your place, I forgot a file in my room. I'll take the car from there."

"Sure. Let's go." I reach into my back pocket for my phone to text Cassie and tell her I'll be late but it's not there.

* * * *

As soon as he's gone, I call Cassie from my landline.

She answers on the fifth ring and sounds groggy. "Leo?"

"Yes. I'm so sorry I'm late. Are you still expecting me?"

"Yes, but no. You didn't come and you didn't answer your phone.

Thought you'd ghosted me again. I poured a glass of wine and drew a bath. I fell asleep in the water."

"That's dangerous, baby."

"I know…But honestly, it's the best sleep I've had all week."

Guilt pricks me. "I'm sorry. It's late. I was going to come over but—"

"You're still coming? Oh my God. For real?"

"Yes, for real Ms. Why." The knot of worry in my chest loosens as I take the first deep breath I've been able to manage all evening. I'm fucking relieved. "I'm on my way."

"I'm so happy to hear you say that, Le—. Wait. Shit. Someone's in my house."

Alarm spikes my pulse. I slip my shoes on and head for the door. "What do you mean someone's in your house?"

"I can hear someone on the stairs. Oh shit. Hold on."

Fear slams my heart against my chest. I break into a run. "I need to call 9-1-1, Cass hold on."

"No, Leo. Wait," she's whispering but her fear is loud and clear. "Please stay with me until I get the door locked."

"Okay. I'm almost there, baby." I sprint down my walkway and head toward her house.

"Shit, shit, he's opening the door to my bedroom, Leo. I can't lock this stupid door," she whispers. "I don't even have any fucking clothes on."

I'm only one house away now, but I can't run fast enough.

"Oh my God. What are *you* doing here?" Cassie yelps. There's a loud clatter before the phone goes dead.

28

Round Two

CASSIE

"Michel?"

"Where is the ring, you thieving bitch?"

"What are you doing here?"

"Give me the ring."

"Never." I bring my knee up, catch him in the groin and then take advantage of his flailing to get him into a headlock.

A pair of handcuffs dangle from his back pocket. My heart seizes. He came here to hurt me.

I grab them and roll over just as his elbow catches me in the ribs.

I double over and his hand fists a clump of my hair. The searing pain makes me howl. But I stay on my feet.

"You're going to give me that ring or I'm going to snap your little neck." He reaches for me, grabs me by the shoulders.

"You've got less than a second to get your hands off her." Leo's voice booms from the doorway. I freeze and so does Michel.

Leo is holding a pistol and his phone. "I've called 9-1-1 but I will shoot your hand off if it's not out of her hair before I get to the end of this sentenc—"

Michel lets me go with a convulsive fling of his hand.

"Put those handcuffs on yourself and toss me the key," Leo commands.

I scramble for the robe on the back of my door and slip it on.

"Now, call my brother. And tell him he's got an hour to get here before I call my friend at CNN."

29

Aftermath

CASSIE

"Are you okay?" Leo sticks his head inside the door of my bedroom. "Can I come in?"

"Of course. And I'm fine. Sore." I sit up in bed and wince at the pain in my hip.

I crawled in as soon as the police were finished taking my statement.

He comes to sit beside me on the bed. "Are the police gone?"

"Yes. They took Michel to formally charge and book him."

"And where's Bismark?"

His face is drawn and he looks exhausted. "He's waiting downstairs."

"What? The police left him here?"

He groans and lays down, covering his eyes with his hands. "He's got diplomatic immunity and is waiting for his escort from the consulate. I just want him to leave in peace. Dealing with Michel will be headache enough."

I nod but I hate that he's going to just walk away like he did nothing. Michel is an asshole but he was hired by him. It seems unfair that he's the only one who is going to pay for what they did.

But I know better than anyone there's a nuance to what's criminal and what's fair. I believe Bismark when he told the police he only sent Michel to steal the ring and that harming me was not his instruction. Whether it's true or he's throwing Michel under the bus, I don't know. But right now, my biggest worry is Leo. I put a hand on his shoulder. "Did you talk to him?"

"Nope." His jaw clenches.

"Has he said anything?"

"Nope."

"Are you going to talk to him? I mean, forget the law, he's your brother."

He drops his hands to his side and opens his eyes. "Only by biology."

My heart aches at the resignation in his voice. "That's not true. You are friends. There's got to be a reason for this. You should talk to him."

30

Father Figure

LEO

Cassie is right. But as soon as I get to the landing of the stairs I freeze.

I can't stop seeing Michel with his hands on Cassie trying to hurt her. Knowing that Biz sent him there made me black with rage.

He and I have had our differences, but this betrayal—apparently a decade in the making—cuts deep.

He's at the kitchen table where I left him. He turns toward me when I enter the kitchen and his blood shot eyes stop me in my tracks. He's been crying. I've never seen him emotional.

What did I miss?

I sit down across from him and our eyes lock. I can see the regret in his, but I don't know what he's sorry for or if it even matters that he is.

"I'm deeply ashamed and sorry Leo." His voice is ragged with emotion.

I look down at my hands and then back at him. "Why did you want it so badly? He left you so much money, power."

He hisses. "Are you kidding? When he was alive, he gave you the only things that mattered to me—freedom, choices. And then when he died, he gave you everything that mattered to him—the house, all that money, and the ring. It should have been mine."

I'm stunned. "Why didn't you just tell me?"

"Why should I have had to?" he shouts.

"Because I'm not a mind reader, asshole." I scoff in disgust. "I would have given it to you. The only thing I wanted from him is the one thing I'll never have."

"What more could you want, Leo?"

"Time. To know him. For him to know me. For him to see me as good enough."

"Oh, Leo."

"Keep your pity. Take the ring and go before I change my mind and call the police again."

"I'm sorry." He looks down at his hands.

I believe him.

"I'm sorry, too."

31

Reunion

Leo

"Damn it." Cassie is asleep by the time I make it back to her bedroom. The lights are on, she's still in her robe and she looks like she fell asleep in the same position I left her in. I'm tempted to crawl in beside her but I'm not sure if she wants me to after what happened tonight.

I pull her blanket up over her shoulders.

"Leo?" Her hand closes around my wrist.

"I'm here." I whisper and sit down next to her.

"Are you okay?"

"I should be asking you that, Cass."

"You already did. And I told you. I'm fine." She reaches around me to turn on the light by her bed.

"It's you I'm worried about. How'd it go with your brother?"

"I gave him the ring."

She sits up straight. "You did what? You said it was irreplaceable."

"It is. But it's not gone. And it meant more to him than it does to me." That certainty is the only reason I let Biz go.

"I'm sorry, Leo."

"I'm not. My father should have given it to him. Now it's where it belongs and there's nothing else they want from me." I look at my hands, bare but for the smart watch on my wrist, and laugh without humor. "I'll probably never hear from him again."

"Will he hear from you?" She asks a question so incisive I wonder if she can read my mind.

"Of course. He's my brother."

She lifts up the corner of her comforter. "Get in here."

"You want me to stay?"

"I need you to stay." She looks at me intently and I climb in.

She presses her front to my back, wraps her arms around my waist, and presses a kiss between my shoulder blades. "Sleep. Tomorrow will be here soon."

I close my eyes and let the exhaustion that followed the rush of adrenaline from this evening have its way.

32

Closure

LEO

Six months later

I'm selling the house in the Seychelles. I haven't been here in ten years and it's been sitting vacant and partially staffed.

Finding a buyer was surprisingly easy. An all-cash offer made it even more so. We close in a week. The movers are coming for the furniture tomorrow. "Are you sure you don't want to stay here tonight?" Cassie asks for the third time.

"Very. I'm ready to move on." I mean that in every way possible.

I have a ring burning a hole in my jacket pocket. I'm going to ask this girl to spend the rest of her life with me.

I can't believe I've been given this second chance.

Selling this house, hiring my former SEAL teammates to work for me, starting a new life in a house with Cassie and Max in Rivers Wilde, all of it is a full circle moment.

I'm finally where I want to be.

"Come on, let's go. Max and your mom are waiting." Cassie takes my hand in hers and we walk out the way we've done everything since we decided to give us a shot—together.

33

Beautiful

CASSIE

I lay in bed, warm and sated in the cottony embrace of the love nest we've made for ourselves and watch him gaze out at the beautiful, lush landscape. I wonder if, like me, he's thinking he's got the most beautiful view in the world.

He's my living dream. And I'm not even talking about that body he treats like a temple and is my favorite place to worship. I'm talking his loyalty, his trust, his courage, his curiosity. I'm in love with his mind and heart and soul. His body is just an extra blessing.

I close my eyes and bathe in the cool breeze that eases the late October heat that's just a taste of what's to come for this little slice of paradise.

I stroke the diamond he put on my ring finger last night and my heart skips a beat.

My wild card has come up aces.

Also from Dylan Allen and 1001 Dark Nights, discover The Mastermind and The Daredevil.

Sign up for the 1001 Dark Nights Newsletter
and be entered to win a Tiffany Key necklace.

There's a contest every month!

Go to www.1001DarkNights.com to subscribe.

**As a bonus, all subscribers can download
FIVE FREE exclusive books!**

Discover 1001 Dark Nights Collection Eleven

DRAGON KISS by Donna Grant
A Dragon Kings Novella

THE WILD CARD by Dylan Allen
A Rivers Wilde Novella

ROCK CHICK REMATCH by Kristen Ashley
A Rock Chick Novella

JUST ONE SUMMER by Carly Phillips
A Dirty Dare Series Novella

HAPPILY EVER MAYBE by Carrie Ann Ryan
A Montgomery Ink Legacy Novella

BLUE MOON by Skye Warren
A Cirque des Moroirs Novella

A VAMPIRE'S MATE by Rebecca Zanetti
A Dark Protectors/Rebels Novella

LOVE HAZARD by Rachel Van Dyken

BRODIE by Aurora Rose Reynolds
An Until Her Novella

THE BODYGUARD AND THE BOMBSHELL by Lexi Blake
A Masters and Mercenaries: New Recruits Novella

THE SUBSTITUTE by Kristen Proby
A Single in Seattle Novella

CRAVED BY YOU by J. Kenner
A Stark Security Novella

GRAVEYARD DOG by Darynda Jones
A Charley Davidson Novella

A CHRISTMAS AUCTION by Audrey Carlan
A Marriage Auction Novella

THE GHOST OF A CHANCE by Heather Graham
A Krewe of Hunters Novella

Also from Blue Box Press:

LEGACY OF TEMPTATION by Larissa Ione
A Demonica Birthright Novel

VISIONS OF FLESH AND BLOOD by Jennifer L. Armentrout and
Ravyn Salvador
A Blood & Ash and Flesh & Fire Compendium

FORGETTING TO REMEMBER by M.J. Rose

TOUCH ME by J. Kenner
A Stark International Novella

BORN OF BLOOD AND ASH by Jennifer L. Armentrout
A Flesh and Fire Novel

MY ROYAL SHOWMANCE by Lexi Blake
A Park Avenue Promise Novel

SAPPHIRE DAWN by Christopher Rice writing as C. Travis Rice
A Sapphire Cove Noveal

LEGACY OF PLEASURE by Larissa Ione
A Demonica Birthright Novel

EMBRACING THE CHANGE by Kristen Ashley
A River Rain Novel

Discover More Dylan Allen

The Mastermind
By Dylan Allen

He lives under a golden spotlight.
I'm shackled to a past that must stay hidden.

Omar Solomon is the king of the comeback.
Ten years ago his career as a star athlete ended in injury and scandal.
He may have traded in his cleats for Gucci loafers, but he's been as victorious in the boardroom as he was on the pitch.

He returns to London, wealthy, influential, and powerful beyond measure.
And he spends every weekend in the pub where I work.
A law student with a night job and a dark past,
I'm hardly the type of woman a man like him would notice.

Or so I thought.

When he offers me a no-strings-attached affair,
I forget all the reasons I should say no.
He's straight out of my dreams—
with a body and a mouth made for sinning.

Our passion turns my gray existence into a vibrant, colorful *life*.
But it has an expiration date.

When his time in London is over, we will be, too.
And it will be for the best.
Because he can never find out who I *really* am.

But my Mastermind has set his sights on a new goal: me.
And this time he's playing for keeps.

* * * *

The Daredevil
By Dylan Allen

"I dare you to let me watch..."

It was the wickedest of propositions, made by the most devilish of men.

It doesn't matter that Tyson Wilde has got a killer smile, wears a suit like it's his job, and oozes spine-tingling sex appeal. I should say no.

Because beneath the surface of that cool, disinterested exterior, lies passion hot enough to burn. I danced too close to it once and have the scars to prove it.

So, on *any* other night, in any other city, and if he'd been even a *fraction* less mouthwatering, I *would* have been able to resist.

But it's my birthday, we're in Paris, and it's *him*.
I can't say no.
I don't want to say no.

And this time, no matter how right we feel together, I won't let myself forget that when this weekend is over, we will be, too.
We're only *pretending* to be lovers to land a deal.
Success will mean a promotion—one I want more than anything.
At least, that's what I thought.

Falling in love was a danger neither Tyson or I saw coming.
And it will cost one of us *everything*.

The Legacy
Rivers Wilde, Book 1
By Dylan Allen

"Toe curling chemistry, a sexy, alpa hero, and a smart heroine! The Legacy is EPIC! Hands down, one of my fav reads this year!" -- Ilsa Madden Mills, Wall Street Journal Bestselling Author.

I hold the keys to a kingdom,
But I covet the key to her heart.
Heir to a fortune, I was born to lead.
After 15 years in exile, a legacy of wealth and power are finally mine to claim.
Falling for the sweet distraction I met at a wedding is the last thing I should do.
The beautiful bombshell is the opposite of everything I should want.
But after a weekend of passion and surprising intimacy, I'm sure she's everything I need.
We come from different worlds.
And the price of entry to mine is steep.
Especially for the proud, independent lawyer who has won my heart.
Before I can convince her we're worth the risk, a lawsuit turns us from lovers to enemies.
I'm forced to choose between the woman I love and the family I'm charged with protecting.
I hold the keys to a kingdom, but I covet the key to her heart;
I'll stop at nothing to have them both.

* * * *

"*Who* is *that?*" I lean over to Cass and whisper without taking my eyes off the tall, well-built man striding into the tent. He looks like he's the sovereign of something—a country, a business, a thousand women in a harem somewhere and is about to declare himself our ruler, and demand we pledge our loyalty or die.

He's even more beautiful in that suit than he was in that hallway this afternoon. I can still feel the soft brush of his fingers on my neck. The way my breath caught in my throat when he'd dragged the pendant up my chest until it nestled into the small hollow at the base of my throat.

His dark, wavy hair is just long enough to curl right at the edge of his crisp white tuxedo shirt. It's unruly and perfectly artless in a way that no human hand, and no amount of pomade, could create. Those silky dark-chocolate waves are the work of God himself.

His profile is strong and bold, his nose prominent and straight. His lips are set in a straight line but I can see their fullness, even in his profile. And Lord Almighty, his jaw. It's chiseled and wide and covered in a beard low enough to be a five o'clock shadow, meticulously groomed, so you can tell it's not.

His tall frame is poured into a black tuxedo that fits him perfectly. Heads turn as he crosses the room. And I can't blame them—not even a little bit. He oozes sex and power. His long strides eat up the floor, and he reaches the lone empty table at the back of the tent quickly. When he's adorned the chair with his glorious body, he turns to face the front of the room where the bridal party is sitting and giving their speeches.

"Who's who?" she asks, and pokes her head around the room. I tug her arm and nod at him.

"Him. Also known as the man of all of my dirty dreams," I purr excitedly, my eyes trained on the finest specimen of man I've ever seen this close up.

"Ohhh," she drawls, eyes widening with interest and props her chin on her hand and ogles him.

"That's Hayes Rivers," the woman on my right says. Cass and I both turn to face her, surprised by her interjection.

"Heir to Kingdom," she says when neither of us respond.

"I knew it. He looks like a king. Which kingdom?" I ask. I'm already imagining myself in a ball gown, crown on my head, walking down some long, red-carpeted aisle where he's waiting at the end.

"No, not *a kingdom*." And just like that, she kills my dream. "*Kingdom* is the name of his family's business. He inherited all the money when he turned twenty-five. And now he's the new Rivers king," she says.

"How old is he now?" I ask, my curiosity overtaking my normal abhorrence for gossip.

"He must be thirty … he's one of the richest men in the freaking world," she exclaims.

"Really? Why's he here?"

"His grandmother is friends with the groom," our little canary says. "I can't believe you've never heard of him. His return to Houston is all anyone's talking about," she says and looks at both of us like we're crazy.

"I don't live in Houston," I say.

"Well, *I* heard ..." Her eyes dart around as if checking for spies and then she leans into us. "Apparently, he had a fight with his ex. And it got *physical*," she grimaces. But her eyes are twinkling. "I'm not one to gossip ..." she says and Cass and I exchange a *yeah, right* look.

"But she was all over the place wearing sunglasses. No one saw her, mind you, and she never said, but it was obvious he roughed her up," she says.

My lawyer hat comes on and my eyes slide away from the delicious man to her. I make sure there's no warmth in them and her silly, careless smile falters.

"That's actually the exact opposite of obvious," I say dismissively.

"Only if you're blind. I mean, yeah, he's nice to look at, but he looks so angry, don't you think?"

I glance at him, and just then, like he knows what she said, his jaw clenches.

"Well, if people were talking about me like this, I might be angry, too," I say and Cass pinches me.

"Well, if you think you know better, you can ignore me. But don't say you weren't warned," she says and turns back to the victim on her other side.

As if I need any warning. I can smell a violent man the minute he enters the room. I grew up with them under the same roof. I watched them do more damage than any of the natural disasters that were a way of life for us in the Mississippi Delta.

I lean toward Cass. "He's staying on our floor," I whisper. I can't take my eyes off him. My whole body is tingling just from looking at him. "Thank you, God," I say, pressing my hands together in gratitude.

Cass laughs. "I mean, he does clean up nicely, but he looks like he'd be more comfortable in a boxing ring than on a dance floor," she says.

"Yes, exactly," I practically purr before I take another sip of my gin and tonic. My thighs clench when I think about how rough things could get.

"His nose doesn't look like it's been broken, though," she muses.

"No one's perfect," I joke, and take a final swig of my drink.

"Enjoy. My fantasy Italian fling is more in the style of Jude Law in the *Talented Mr. Ripley*. He looks like he could eat Jude Law in a single bite."

"Or me," I drawl with a wink and stand up. I run my hands down my dress.

Cass grabs my arm and yanks me back down in my seat. "Where in the world are you going? You are *not* going to approach him," she says as if scandalized.

I glance over at her and grin, because I am *so* going to approach him.

"You never approach anyone. You're still getting over Nigel. Who *are* you?" she asks, green eyes wide with surprise.

"I'm Confidence Ryan, and I'm about to go climb my very own Mt. Olympus," I say with a suggestive waggle of my eyebrows.

"Are you drunk?" she asks when I start to stand up again.

"Yes, but so what?" I say.

"You'll regret it in the morning," she frets.

"Maybe …" I shrug.

"This isn't you." She peers up at me.

"Again, so what?" I shrug off her questions. "I'm in Italy. I'm single. And I think that if I'm ready to walk over and put my ass on a table for another man to make a meal of me, then I might be over Nigel," I say.

"True facts," she says with an enthusiastic nod.

"And if I have regrets … then, at least it will be for something worth regretting. I want to know what that kind of regret feels like," I say in a moment of rare vulnerability.

"Okay," she says, relenting in her attempts to stop me. Even if she doesn't sound convinced.

"Just be safe. Get your own drinks and drop your glass so it shatters if you need a rescue," she says and takes a sip of her drink.

"I won't be breaking any glasses. If I need a rescue, I'll do it myself." A sudden bolt of doubt flashes through my mind.

This *is* very unlike me.

About Dylan Allen

Wall Street Journal and USA Today Bestselling Author, Dylan Allen writes compelling, dramatic, emotional romances with exceptional, diverse characters you'll root for and never forget.

A self-proclaimed happily ever junkie, she loves creating stories where her characters find a love worth fighting for. When she isn't writing or reading, eating, or cooking, Dylan indulges her wanderlust by planning her next globe-trotting adventure.

Dylan was born in Accra, Ghana (West Africa) but was raised in Houston, Texas. Dylan is a proud graduate of Tufts University, Howard University School of Law and the London School of Economics and Political Science. After twenty years of adventure and wild oat sowing, Dylan, her amazing husband and two incredible children returned to Baltimore where they now make their home.

* * * *

I love to hear from readers! email me at Dylan@dylanallenbooks.com

Are you on Facebook? Join my private reader group, Dylan's Day Dreamers. It's where I spend most of my time online and it's a lot of fun!

On Behalf of 1001 Dark Nights,
Liz Berry, M.J. Rose, and Jillian Stein would like to thank ~

Steve Berry
Doug Scofield
Benjamin Stein
Kim Guidroz
Chelle Olson
Tanaka Kangara
Asha Hossain
Chris Graham
Jessica Saunders
Stacey Tardif
Dylan Stockton
Kate Boggs
Richard Blake
and Simon Lipskar

Made in the USA
Middletown, DE
19 March 2024